Turned by a Tiger

Felicity Heaton

ETERNAL MATES SERIES

Kissed by a Dark Prince
Claimed by a Demon King
Tempted by a Rogue Prince
Hunted by a Jaguar
Craved by an Alpha
Bitten by a Hellcat
Taken by a Dragon
Marked by an Assassin
Possessed by a Dark Warrior
Awakened by a Demoness
Haunted by the King of Death
Turned by a Tiger
Tamed by a Tiger – Coming in 2017
Treasured by a Tiger – Coming in 2017

Find out more at: www.felicityheaton.co.uk

CHAPTER 1

"Shit."

Talon's knees hit the tarmac with a bone-crunching jolt and he sagged forwards, breath sawing from his lips as he fought to remain conscious and drive the pain back as it swarmed him, threatening to drag him into the waiting darkness. He couldn't pass out here. They would find him.

He wearily lifted his head and growled low in his throat at the effort it took to do such a simple thing now. Not good.

He gazed down at his lap and then his trembling left hand as he pulled it away from his bare stomach. His hand wobbled and blurred, and he blinked hard, fighting to clear his vision and refusing to let the pain ricocheting through him, a bone-deep savage onslaught that wouldn't abate, overcome him. The streetlight off to his right caught the thick layer of blood on his hand and turned it black and shiny.

"Fuck," he growled through clenched teeth and tears stung his eyes.

He forced his right hand up and scrubbed it across his face, rubbing them away.

No damn way he was going to cry, no matter how dire things looked.

He wouldn't give up.

He pressed his damp right hand into the gritty road and pushed himself onto his feet. Lightning flash through him, fire licking along the length of the wound across his stomach, and he gritted his teeth so hard they creaked, but he kept going, kept pushing, kept refusing to just lie down and die.

Death would be a mercy, one that probably wouldn't find him before the bastards hunting him did.

Talon staggered onto his bare feet, stumbled a few steps and grunted as his right shoulder smashed into the wall that lined the narrow alley.

Awareness prickled down his spine and he looked over his left shoulder, his long beard scraping his skin and his shaggy black hair falling to obscure his eyes. He didn't have the strength to push it out of his face.

Or the time.

They were coming.

Closing in now.

Dammit.

He had to keep moving. He was close.

The world wobbled around him, losing colour at times, as he stumbled forwards, clutching his stomach with his left hand and wincing with each laboured step. That damned lightning and fire zapped and danced through him with each shift of his body that disturbed the worst of his injuries, forcing him to breathe shallowly in an effort to keep it at bay.

1

Gods-fucking-dammit.

It wasn't going to end here.

His right ankle gave out and the tarmac loomed in his vision again, but this time he managed to catch himself at the last moment.

Would've been a triumph if he hadn't face-planted into a brick wall instead.

He rested against it, giving himself a moment, aware that if he kept pushing this hard he was going to pass out and that would land him back in their hands.

That prickling sensation came again, warning him they were narrowing the search, growing closer with every moment he stood still. He had to keep moving, even if it was only inches at a time. He leaned against the wall, using it for support and clawing his way along it with his right hand, his fingertips aching as he dragged his weight.

His muscles trembled beneath his skin, on the verge of going liquid as his strength drained away.

Another sensation joined the first.

One of dread that hounded him as he pulled himself forwards with dogged determination.

There were more than night shadows behind him.

There was death.

It was stalking him like the hunters, waiting for that moment when he gave in.

Never.

Talon ground his teeth and staggered forwards, calling on all of his strength and refusing to give up. He hadn't given up when the hunters had caught him. He hadn't given up all the times they had demanded he shift into his tiger form and then tortured him with cattle prods to force him to turn back. He hadn't given up when they had left him naked and bleeding in that infernal cage or all the times they had dragged him back to his cell, letting their other captives witness him at his weakest.

He would never give up.

He kept inching forwards, the pain mounting inside him stealing his breath as it reached a new crescendo and fresh warmth spilled across his left hand, his life draining from him. Couldn't give up. Wouldn't.

Talon growled and pushed onwards, near-blind as fire blazed inside him, devouring his strength and setting every nerve in his body alight. Instinct drove and guided him, a deep desire to survive that lived within all feline shifter species, as strong and undeniable as the need to defend their territory.

Something he was deeply aware of as he finally reached the end of the alley and his destination.

He stared across the narrow road to the red-brick warehouse.

He shouldn't be here, but he was desperate, had nowhere else to go and no hope of surviving if he couldn't convince the shifter who owned the building to give him sanctuary.

The chance of that happening was slim, about as slender as him surviving the night.

But he had to risk it.

Underworld was his only hope now.

He checked the silent street in both directions, studying the shadows to make sure he wasn't being watched, and then limped across it to the other side, slumped against the wall and clawed himself forwards, towards the broad door beneath the unlit neon sign.

The scent of shifter hit him hard, flowing from a torn up piece of wood beside the door, the owner's calling card and a message to other male cat shifters in their prime.

A warning to stay away.

He couldn't.

He reached the door and rested, breathing hard and fighting the nerves rising inside him to mingle with the pain. His limited senses stretched around him, ears pricking as he listened for a sign of life—both inside the building and outside it with him. There was no one in the streets around him, but inside were two heartbeats, not far on the other side of the door.

Talon pulled his hand away from his stomach and banged his fist on the door.

It swung open the moment he made contact and he lost balance, falling inside to land in a heap on the floor.

"We're closed," a deep gruff male voice called from the darkness. "I thought you'd locked up?"

Talon ignored the male and crawled forwards, dragging himself with both hands now, desperation driving him and urging him onwards, into the gloom. He growled. He was moving too slowly, the distance between him and the door not growing quickly enough. He needed to go faster.

Pain shot through him, his ears ringing with it and heart labouring in response, and he clutched his stomach with his left hand again, grunting as he fought it. When it eased, he pushed up on his right hand and shuffled forwards, holding his stomach with his other hand. The scent of his own blood filled his nostrils and his vision wobbled again.

Dammit.

He pressed harder with his left hand, trying to stem the bleeding. It wasn't slowing.

Silence fell like a thick shroud.

Eyes landed on him, intent and focused.

The air shifted and a growl echoed through the enormous room, unholy and vicious.

A warning he felt all the way down to his bones.

To his soul.

His hope ended here.

The shifter was going to kill him.

3

CHAPTER 2

Sherry's bottom hit the top of the low wine refrigerator as Kyter suddenly vaulted the black bar that ran almost the entire length of one wall of Underworld. She quickly set down the cloth she had been using to dry the last of the glasses and rushed forwards, running down the narrow walkway behind the bar and reaching the end just as Kyter hauled the stranger off his knees and onto his feet, and landed a hard right hook across his jaw.

The big guy growled through the thick black beard covering the lower half of his face and hit the wall close to her, slid down it and landed on his butt on the tacky floor.

"Kyter," Sherry snapped, but her boss wasn't listening.

His eyes glowed golden in the low light as he stalked towards the man, muscles tense beneath his white dress shirt, coiled in readiness.

She looked down at the newcomer.

The poor bastard wasn't in any shape to fight, had shocked her when she had seen him dragging himself into the club. At first, she had figured him for a local homeless drunk, with his wild shaggy black hair that brushed his nape, ragged thick beard, and his lack of clothes, but the way her boss had reacted told her he was something else.

Another cat shifter.

Kyter often lost his shit when male shifters came into the club unannounced and uninvited.

Apparently it was a territory thing.

Sherry didn't think this man was here to fight Kyter for his perceived territory though.

Blood covered his bare chest, outlining some of the hard compact muscles and concealing the rest. It drenched his left arm from the elbow down too, and had stuck his loose black cotton trousers to his left thigh.

The man lifted amber eyes to lock with Kyter's golden ones and bared his fangs on a snarl.

Kyter didn't back off.

He grabbed the man by his throat, pulled him up the wall and punched him again, bristling with aggression as he growled right in the man's face and bared his own emerging fangs.

"Kyter!" She would keep shouting his damned name until she got through to him or her voice gave out. "Kyter!"

He still refused to heed her and she flinched as he went to town on the poor bastard, hitting him with a low blow to his stomach that had fresh blood rolling down his hip and a pained growl leaving his lips. The man sagged but Kyter held him up, shoved harder against his throat.

Something inside Sherry snapped, and she lifted the section of bar in front of her, driven to intervene, but stopped dead when the injured man roared.

A wave of prickles rushed down her spine and the hairs on the back of her neck stood on end as her heart thundered in response to that feral and wild sound.

In a move she couldn't track, he launched Kyter across the room, sending her boss slamming into the wall. Kyter hit the deck but was on his feet a heartbeat later, launching back at the newcomer.

What had him so damned intent on killing the bastard?

Was the man a jaguar too?

Normally when Kyter got pissy because another cat shifter had come into the club, he managed to hold himself together and keep his irritation to a series of low growls and death glares, and the odd kicking out.

There had been one time when he had really lost his shit though, had ended up in a brawl that had emptied the busy club.

That time, it had been a fellow jaguar that had rolled in.

The injured man caught Kyter as he tackled him and wrestled with him, his muscles bunching and bulging as he strained against Kyter and fought to subdue him. A low growl curled from his lips as he got the upper hand.

Kyter snarled right back and pushed harder, managed to twist his right arm free and smash his fist into the man's face.

The man staggered towards Sherry, going down the whole time, and she flinched as his face smacked off the end of the bar and he ended up in a tangled heap on the floor, his left arm hooked through the legs of one of the bar stools.

Kyter was on him in the blink of an eye, pounding his chest and face with hard blows. The man roared and bucked up, closed his fist around the stool and swung it at Kyter's head.

Her boss grunted as it impacted, fell to his left and rolled onto his feet. Blood trickled down from a gash above his right eyebrow, dripping into his eye and onto his cheek. He growled and swiped his hand across it, and was on the other man before she could even attempt to track his movements.

The man flew past her and crashed into the wall just ten foot from her, leaving a huge dent in the black plaster. He landed on his face and lay there, so still she was sure he was dead.

Kyter prowled towards him, clearly convinced that he wasn't and determined to finish him off.

He had to be another jaguar.

The man twitched and then he was gone, leaped clear just as Kyter landed where he had been.

Her gaze zipped to the man and her blue eyes widened as beautiful amber fur striped with thick black bands rippled over his bare chest and down his arms.

Not a jaguar.

A tiger.

He growled, bearing huge canines.

Kyter twisted and leaped again, springing across the gap to land on the man's chest. The man caught him and they went down hard in a tangle of limbs. She winced again as Kyter managed to get on top and landed a solid left hook that snapped the tiger's head around and made his teeth clack together so hard she heard them.

The big tiger snarled and shook his head, and she had the terrible feeling that he was going to pass out.

Or die.

She couldn't let him die.

That sensation went through her like a thunderclap, lighting her up inside with a weird sort of energy, a need that drove her to obey it.

Tiger rolled and got the upper hand on Kyter for all of a second.

Her boss pressed his feet into the man's stomach and kicked, sending him sailing through the air again. She squeezed her eyes shut as he hit the bar, bending backwards over it, and barked out a pained whimper before collapsing on the floor and scattering several bar stools.

Kyter dragged a hand over his wild sandy hair and advanced.

Tiger didn't move.

She had to do something.

Her boss was going to kill him if she kept standing back and let things continue.

That lightning arced through her again, that dangerous need that demanded she obey it.

She had to protect the tiger.

Aware that she might get hurt, that placing herself between two cat shifters was madness and beyond a risky move, she swiftly rounded the bar, because she was equally as aware she had to save the tiger.

That only she could save him.

Kyter snarled and swung at the male, his claws cutting through the air.

Sherry leaped between them, splaying her arms out at her sides to block his path to the tiger.

She flinched away, heart rocketing, blood pounding and dizziness setting in as she struggled not to pass out from the fear that blasted through her, fear that this was the end and defending the tiger had just got her killed instead of him.

The expected blow didn't come.

She slowly cracked her eyes open and they widened as she saw Kyter's extended claws in the corner of her field of vision.

Her boss stood just inches from her, breathing so hard she thought the buttons of his white shirt might pop off at any moment. His golden eyes glowed in the dim light from behind the bar, drilling into her with a question, a demand to know what had possessed her and made her leap between him and the tiger.

She wasn't sure.

She just hadn't been able to stand idle any longer, letting him fight when he was wounded, weak from his injuries. It wasn't fair, and he hadn't done anything to deserve such a brutal attack from her boss.

Sherry backed off a step, moving one closer to the tiger, but maintained her pose, blocking Kyter's way to the man.

Kyter huffed and eased back a step too, and raked long fingers through his hair as he breathed hard, clearly fighting the urge to get at the tiger and take him down.

"Reining it in." He held his hands up at his sides when she continued to watch him, and even went as far as moving back another two steps.

He muttered something under his breath and began pacing. She had seen Kyter do that enough times to know to give him space. He had a habit of working off energy by pacing.

It was a cat thing.

She had seen their resident snow leopard shifter, Cavanaugh, use the same trick when his mate had wound him up or someone had dared to look at her.

Sherry looked over her shoulder at the tiger where he knelt behind her, doubled over and clutching his stomach, his black head bent so she couldn't see his face.

She had the feeling he hadn't wandered here by mistake, and hadn't come looking for a fight.

She had a feeling that he was looking for salvation.

Protection.

He lifted his head and she sucked in a breath as bright amber eyes met hers and heat curled through her, a fire that only grew in intensity as a low growl curled from his bloodstained lips.

The club whooshed past her and she gasped as she flew backwards. She stumbled and grunted as the hand suddenly clamped around her right wrist hauled her upwards again, jerking her forwards and slamming her into a broad masculine back.

Kyter.

He held her behind him, shielding her with his body.

Why?

She hadn't been in danger.

Not physical danger anyway.

She was no cat shifter but she had the undeniable sensation that growl hadn't been a show of aggression.

It had been a show of possession.

A sign that even in his weakened state, knocking on Death's door, this mysterious tiger shifter wanted her.

Sherry eased out of Kyter's shadow, curiosity seizing control of her, filling her with a need to see the tiger. "What do you want?"

Those stunning amber eyes locked on her again, startling in their intensity. They seemed to brighten, glowing gold in their centres as he studied her. He wanted her. It was right there in his eyes for her to read, unmistakeable and undeniable.

Kyter snagged his attention again by moving a step forwards.

Tiger bristled, growling and snapping huge fangs, and then a flash of regret crossed his handsome rough face when Kyter huffed and folded his arms across his chest. The man shrank back, eased onto his butt on the floor and slumped wearily against the black bar.

When his chin dropped and his shoulders trembled, she lowered her eyes to his chest and the wounds that littered it, and then continued downwards to his stomach. The gash that darted across it was deep, still dripping blood.

"Who did this to you?" she whispered.

His lips moved soundlessly at first, repeating a single word, but then he managed to put his voice behind it.

"Archangel."

Sherry found that hard to believe. The look on Kyter's face when she glanced at him said he did too.

"Archangel aren't in the habit of taking innocents, so what did you do to get on the wrong side of them?" Kyter curled a lip at the tiger and fire flared in his golden eyes.

Tiger struggled, managed to get a few syllables out but nothing that resembled a word. His head drooped again and he fought to lift it, but failed and his chin almost hit his chest. The need to know what had brought him to them and who had done such terrible things to him washed away, replaced with a more powerful need to take care of him.

If they didn't help him soon, it would be too late.

"He needs medical attention." Sherry ignored the gruff look that Kyter shot her, one that said he didn't want to help the tiger until he knew everything. She glared at her boss, giving him her best withering stare, the one she had worked hard to perfect since entering employment at Underworld over a decade ago. "We can ask him questions when he can actually talk without passing out… and maybe we'll get answers then."

"I want answers now." Kyter's deep voice had that hard edge to it, the one he always used when laying down the law with his staff. It wasn't going to work on her. "I won't allow a dangerous shifter in my club. If Archangel comes, I'll hand the son of a bitch over."

"No!" There was such desperation, so much fear in that single word as the tiger jolted forwards, that she couldn't stop herself from reacting, even when she knew it might cost her job.

Or more.

She stepped between him and Kyter again, heart racing against her ribs and a tiny part of her screaming not to do this, that it was dangerous and foolish, and blurted, "I'll take him to my place and that way the club will be safe."

Kyter's golden eyes narrowed on her, but it was the feel of the tiger's eyes drilling into the back of her head that held her awareness, making her want to look over her shoulder at him and answer his silent question.

Yes, she was crazy and she was offering to take him home with her.

She had lost her fucking mind.

"I won't put you in danger, Sherry. I'm not going to let you take him," Kyter snapped and shook his head, his golden eyes daring her to go against what sounded a lot like an order to her.

He had hated it when she had decided to move out two years ago, finding her own place so she could have a little space away from the club, a home to call her own, but in the end he had supported her.

Mostly because she had cited his and Cavanaugh's tendency to snore so loudly she barely got any sleep in her small apartment in the club, and had then made him squirm by making up stuff about how her sex life had taken a huge nosedive because she couldn't take a man up to her apartment without Kyter prowling around like some terrifying big brother and scaring them away.

Her sex life had been dead on arrival for a long time, but Kyter didn't need to know that.

She knew he wanted to protect her, loved that about him, but sometimes she had to stand on her own two feet.

"I'm taking him." She crossed her arms over her chest, mimicking him.

He huffed. "No. What if he hurts you?"

The tiger growled at that, as if the fact Kyter had dared to even think him capable of such a thing had pissed him off.

She looked back over her shoulder at him and realised she had no reason to believe he wouldn't hurt her. It was a gut feeling, and her gut hadn't failed her yet. It had brought her to this place at the lowest point in her life when she had run away from home, and told her to stick around when Kyter had offered to take her in like some stray, and again when she had discovered she wasn't working for humans.

Now it was telling her that this man was innocent, and if she didn't help him, he would die.

"What if he did something terrible to make Archangel capture him?" Kyter's words were low spoken, cautious and deadly serious.

Sherry stared at the tiger, right into his amber eyes. "What if he didn't?"

She looked back at Kyter when he huffed again.

"It wouldn't be the first time Archangel had taken someone innocent. Cavanaugh's brother Harbin was captured by them… and what about Loke?" She had known of Archangel's existence from the night she had discovered Kyter was in fact a jaguar shifter and he had sat her down and told her everything he could about his world, and the truth about the one that surrounded her.

Back then, Archangel had been righteous, had reinvented itself as a champion for the fae and other immortal species after a bloody history with them. It had hunted only the immortals who were a danger to their own kind. Things had been changing though, and she knew even Kyter had his doubts about the hunter organisation now.

Kyter looked as if he wanted to argue with her, but then his face softened on a sigh and he shook his head. She was winning.

"I'm starting to get the feeling that Archangel aren't all they appear to be... that they do bad as well as good... and you know you are too." She pressed her advantage, seeing victory within her reach and unwilling to back down now.

Kyter would relent, and the tiger would be spared.

Saved.

That desire, that deep instinct and need that had sparked to life inside her when she had seen him close to falling, would be satisfied at last.

She would have protected him.

Her boss huffed again and glared at the tiger, who didn't bite. He remained still behind her, so still in fact that she had to glance over her shoulder at him again to check he was still with them. He stared up at her, those amber eyes bright but dull with pain at the same time. His left hand shook against his bare stomach. Blood trickled from between his strong fingers.

"It's my choice," she whispered and then added with more conviction as she turned to face Kyter again, "I'm going to help him no matter what you have to say about it."

He frowned at her. "There's no way you're walking out of here with three hundred pounds of half-dead tiger and making it home, not if Archangel are hunting him."

He had a point, and she didn't exactly have a solution to offer him. She wracked her brain, trying to think of something that would satisfy him enough that he wouldn't revert back to refusing to let her go with the tiger in tow.

Kyter tunnelled his fingers through his sandy hair, tousling the already worry-ruffled locks further, and heaved a long sigh that spoke volumes— tomes—about how he felt about what he was about to suggest and what she was doing.

"I'll ask Io for help."

The hope that had been fading inside her burst back to life like a phoenix from the ashes, but she didn't have a chance to thank Kyter for deciding to help her.

He pivoted on his heel and strode towards the door in the right wall of the nightclub beyond the bar, muttering, "Wait here while I ask Io."

She was going to have to thank Iolanthe a thousand times over if she agreed to help out, and Kyter too for thinking of a way to get her home with the tiger without Archangel seeing her. She really hadn't thought things through when she had rushed to his aid, acting like some white knight to his damsel in distress.

At least this way, the tiger could heal and Kyter could get the answers he wanted about Archangel.

Answers she wanted too.

She wanted to know why they had done such horrible things to him.

Kyter paused at the black metal door and looked back at her, concern lighting his eyes and echoing in his deep voice.

"Will you be alright?"

Sherry nodded.

He lingered a moment and then punched in the security code, twisted the silver knob and opened the door. It closed with a bang that echoed through the club and jangled her nerves, making her deeply aware of the fact she was now alone with the tiger.

She looked down at him.

He lifted his head, those piercing amber eyes rising to meet hers again.

Sherry stared down into them, drowning in their liquid gold depths.

Heat travelled through her limbs and warmed the space behind her breast that had been cold for so long.

At least she thought she would be alright.

CHAPTER 3

Everything was hazy, wrought with pain and fire, but Talon was deeply aware as he gazed up at the female standing over him in the large dimly-lit nightclub, a female who had defended him, that she was something to him.

Something powerful.

Something beautiful.

Incredible.

But also something impossible.

She was human.

A grunt left him as the pain blazing in his side grew stronger again, sending a fierce wave of agony rolling through him that tried to steal consciousness from his grasp. He fought it and the encroaching darkness, afraid that if he succumbed to it that he would pass out and the beauty standing before him would disappear, and when he woke she would be gone.

Nothing more than a memory.

Or a figment of his imagination.

She leaned past him, over the bar, and when she moved back to stand before him again, a dark towel hung from her right hand.

He opened his mouth, but nothing more than a croak came out of his bruised throat. He grimaced and tried again, pushing words past his cracked lips.

"Are you real?"

Pale pink full lips curled into a soft smile that reached her dazzling blue eyes and she crouched before him, a fearless and alluring little thing, and whispered, "I am. Rest easy."

She took his hand, her touch electric, sending a fierce sizzle along his skin, and placed the towel against his left side. He stared at her as she put his hand over it and pressed down, her palm warm against the back of his hand.

"Keep pressure on it." She glanced up into his eyes. "Io will be here soon. She'll help me take you somewhere safe."

Somewhere safe.

Talon wasn't sure that was possible, but he didn't want to tell her that, because he was lucid enough to understand that this somewhere safe she spoke of was her home, and he would be alone with her.

With this mesmerising and bewitching mortal.

His cat prowled beneath the surface of his skin, restless and hungry despite the pain that kept it held within him, caged there. Normally when he was injured, he had no inclination to shift, but something about her made him want to turn all tiger on her and drive her into submission.

There was fire in her, a spark that fascinated him, one he hadn't seen in a female in a long time and had never considered a mere human could possess.

He had never realised before meeting this female that humans could have so much courage and strength, had been oblivious to it, believing them all weak creatures, frail and cowardly, who would last five seconds in a world of shifters, fae and demons if those species decided to make this world theirs.

The way she had stepped between him and the jaguar, placing herself in harm's way to protect him.

A stranger.

It fascinated him.

Changed his entire opinion of her species.

Shattered it in fact, so the truth could shine through.

There were humans who were brave, strong of heart and body, ready to stand and fight for the sake of species far more powerful than they were.

There were also humans who were strong of heart and body, and ready to enslave and torture the very same species in their quest for knowledge and power.

Archangel.

He growled low in his throat, a reaction he couldn't contain as he thought about them, one born of anger and grief, of suffering and a desperate need for vengeance.

He narrowed his focus back to the female, shutting out the memories of his time in Archangel's hands, not strong enough to face them right now.

He was in her hands now, and he hoped she would be gentler with him than Archangel had been, would show him that not all humans despised his kind.

Those pretty blush lips parted to reveal straight white teeth, and then she froze and looked off to her left, leaving him wondering what she had wanted to say while staring so deeply into his eyes that he was left feeling empty as she tore her eyes from his, as if her gaze had stolen a piece of him.

He looked in that direction too and frowned as a slender, tall female with a regal air strode towards him beside the bar, skin-tight black armour hugging her figure. She twisted her sleek fall of black hair into a knot at the back of her head and shoved a silver pin through it with an air of irritation that said she wanted to stick it in someone.

Who?

The jaguar following on her heels or him for coming here and disturbing the peace?

The jaguar snarled at him, baring fangs, and Talon got the warning loud and clear.

He looked away from the female. The jaguar's mate.

She wasn't a shifter though.

Immortal, yes, but not a shifter. How was she meant to help the human take him to her home?

The answer hit him when he risked a glance at the female and noticed something about her.

Pointed ears.

An elf?

Talon had never met one before.

A hazy notion hovered at the edges of his mind, a feeling that crept in and slowly came into focus as he tugged at it. There had been an elf at Archangel. He vaguely remembered there being one. Or had it been two?

They hadn't been prisoners though. He frowned, trying to put the pieces together, a growing feeling gnawing at his gut as he focused, becoming clearer at the same time as his memories.

They had been guests. He had caught their scent once, when being dragged from the cage and taken to his cell. He had overheard the guards muttering about working with the fae.

It had surprised him then, and it rocked him now.

The elves were allies of Archangel.

They were in league with them.

The female meant him harm. She meant to hand him over to them so they could lock him up again, could torture him. For what purpose? Why were the elves helping Archangel with their terrible experiments?

He wasn't sure, but he wouldn't rest until he knew, and he wouldn't allow this female to come anywhere near him.

He wouldn't go back.

"Traitor," he snarled through emerging fangs and used his right hand to push himself away from her, shuffling on his backside towards the exit.

He didn't make it far before the pain became so intense he couldn't breathe.

The vicious roar of the jaguar sounded around him, echoing through the empty club.

Darkness swept up and he pushed it back, refused to let it take him and leave him vulnerable when he needed to fight.

Needed to escape.

As the pain abated, and the risk of passing out faded, the world drifted back together with the feel of hands on his forearms, restraining him.

Hands that held him firmly, but didn't belong to the jaguar.

Talon opened his eyes and looked at the delicate hands on him, touching his bare flesh, stained with his blood. Not strong hands. Not immortal and unyielding, able to break his bones if he tried to escape.

They were tender, their touch comforting, their grip meant to restrain him with their gentle understanding and not force.

He lifted his eyes to meet blue ones.

The mortal.

She crouched before him, close to him, so close he could feel her heat and her scent rolled over him, sweet like honey and vanilla. Gods, he wanted to drown in that smell, wanted to roll in it and cover himself in it, to rub against her so he would smell of only her.

And she would smell of him.

A touch of colour darkened her cheeks, but she didn't release him and didn't move to distance herself.

She stood her ground, noble and courageous, determined to bend him to her will.

"Iolanthe won't hurt you," she whispered softly, her voice a gentle breeze that carried away his fear and his panic, and part of his pain, sedating him and easing his tiger side. That part of him settled, the desire to fight and flee fading as he looked into her eyes and let her words wash over him. She glanced at the elf. "Will you, Io?"

He looked there too, in time to see the elf nod.

"I'm no traitor... and I don't have a clue what he's blathering about. Is he delusional?"

The female had a way of insulting people with barely a handful of words that he had never encountered in his three hundred plus years.

The jaguar standing guard beside her slid her a look, rolled his eyes and sighed in a way that said he had given up trying to iron out this particular wrinkle in her personality and was just going to roll with it now.

"Elves work with Archangel now," Talon muttered, and didn't fight the human as she helped him back into a sitting position with his shoulders resting against the front of the bar.

The elf shrugged. "I know. My brother spent some time there with the prince."

Talon's guard went back up so fast it made him dizzy, the sudden spike in adrenaline sending strength surging through him and rousing his tiger instincts, bringing them back to the fore.

She spoke of the two guests.

She knew them.

She was in league with them.

"You mean me harm," he barked and pushed the human away from him, launched a hand up to grab the rail around the bar above his head, and hauled himself onto his feet. He growled at the elf, his fangs punching long from his gums and fur rushing over his shoulders and arms as he called on more of his strength. His tiger instincts roared it was a trap. "You mean to hand me over to your brother and your brother will hand me to Archangel... and return me to the nightmare."

A wave of dizziness, stronger than before, crashed over him and his knees buckled.

The little human caught him under his arms and steadied him, and he froze with his back pressing against the cold brass bar and her firm body warming his front.

Talon gazed down at her, awareness of the world around him washing away again.

Gods, she was achingly beautiful.

"It won't happen." Her soft voice offered the comfort he needed, soothing the raging beast inside him, placating it and subduing him with a speed that left him shaken.

What power did this female have over him?

It was dangerous.

He was dangerous.

As much as he wanted her, as deeply as he needed her, he couldn't have her.

The sandy-haired shifter casually leaned his left hip against the bar and folded his arms across his chest. "It might if he doesn't start cooperating… but it will be a jaguar shifter returning him by kicking him out of this club and leaving him on the curb for Archangel to find. I still think he did something to make him deserve being there."

"No." He lunged forwards, filled with a need to grab the jaguar and fight him to make him listen and believe him.

He hit an obstacle, a soft wall of feminine curves and enticing scent mingled with comforting warmth that stopped him in his tracks.

His gaze dropped to the mortal's again.

His strength left him, as if her calming presence sucked it out of him, tearing down the barriers and the need to fight, twisting it into a need to surrender and give in. To let go.

To let her be strong for him.

He shook his head, but he couldn't shake the memories as easily. They clung to him, refusing to let him go, torturing him with the past.

"I did nothing," he whispered brokenly, lost in her blue eyes, almost able to feel the warmth of the sun on his bare skin as he gazed into their endless azure depths. "They took me… and others… a night raid… a fae town. The others…"

Darkness closed in around the blue and he swallowed hard.

Her hands pressed against his sides, gentle pressure that kept him with her as she softly said, "Don't push yourself. You need to rest."

"The others…"

She slowly shook her head. "There's nothing you can do for them as you are now."

He knew that. He had barely escaped with his life, might have been dying on the curb outside if not for the female standing in front of him, gently holding him. He knew it but it didn't stop the need from ruling him, pushing him to do something, even when he didn't have the strength.

It would be suicide.

"You going to let it go for now and focus on healing?" She canted her head, causing her long blonde ponytail to sway across her shoulders.

He ached to brush his fingers through the silken threads, lift them to his nose and inhale her scent. Gods, she had such power over him, and he didn't really know her. His tiger side purred at the thought of rubbing against her hair, smelling it and then lowering his head to tease the nape of her neck with his teeth and lave it with his tongue.

Talon nodded slowly, a little lost in his fantasy, in the seductive proposition of surrendering to her and his animal instincts.

"Are we going, or do you want to go all kitty on her and get it over with?" The sharp female voice snapped him back to the room and he looked off to his right, at the elf where she stood with her hands planted against her hips and a sour look on her face.

How the hell had she known his thoughts?

Elves weren't psychic.

The hard set of the jaguar's face said he had picked them up too, or at least knew the look he had been sporting well enough to know what he wanted to do. The male's golden eyes narrowed on his, filled with a warning and a promise of pain if he dared to lay a hand on the human, let alone run his tongue over the deliciously tempting nape of her neck.

The human blinked at both of them, and then at him, a beautifully confused edge to her expression. He wasn't about to spell things out for her. If she didn't know what they were talking about, that was all good with him.

She canted her head again and looked as if she was going to ask.

Iolanthe moved forwards, silent on the dark floorboards even though she wore heeled boots that looked as if they had been made for the express purpose of kicking arse. "You want some blood? It'll accelerate the healing process."

She offered her wrist.

The jaguar growled low and bared his fangs, leaving Talon in little doubt that taking the offered blood would end in his death and not his salvation.

He shook his head, politely turning her down, and pretended to ignore that baser side of his nature that growled at him to take the human's blood instead.

Human blood had no healing properties.

His more animal side didn't care about such trivial facts. It wanted to bite her. He wanted to bite her. His eyes betrayed him and shifted to her neck, to the back of it, just below her hairline, and he ached inside, burned with a need to sink his fangs in there and mark her.

Not going to happen.

She was human.

"Just need rest," he muttered and looked down, meaning to check his wounds.

He got an eyeful of cleavage instead. Fuck. He hadn't realised how pressed up against him the mortal was now as she supported him. The urge to drink his fill of the way her breasts were squashed up in her white shirt, and against him, lasted all of a second before it shattered under the blow of a single realisation.

He was bleeding all over her.

He shifted his left hand, swallowed hard as his fingers pressed against her ribs beneath her right breast and she gasped, a wicked little sound that stirred his blood.

"Bleeding," he rasped, his words hollow in his ears, distant as he stared down at her and grew aware of every place their bodies touched.

She blinked, looked down at her chest where it pressed against his bare stomach, froze for a second in which he could feel her heartbeat pick up, and then she was two feet away from him and busying herself with her ruined shirt.

Talon sagged against the bar and fought a wave of nausea as he was forced to hold his weight up on his own. Damn. The little human was stronger than she looked, must have been bearing almost half of his weight for him. For a moment, he had foolishly believed he had been regaining his strength.

Fucking idiot.

His knees gave out, the human gasped again, and he grunted as he hit the floor.

"Shit," she muttered and was beside him in a flash, her hands on his shoulders, pushing him back into a sitting position. "Sorry."

He wasn't sure why she was apologising.

She caught him under his arms and tried to haul him onto his feet. He would have helped her, but the world was spinning around him, blurring together into colourful streaks that made him dizzy.

"I'll send word to my brother," the elf said and he sensed her moving closer as the ground pitched beneath him. "Prince Loren will want to know everything you have to say about Archangel. If they're up to something, he won't stand for it."

It was a relief to hear that, and not only because the elves being on the side of Archangel would sway the odds in their favour if it came to a war between the immortal species and the mortal hunter organisation.

It was a relief because he couldn't detect any hint of a lie in what she had said. She was telling him the truth. He always knew when someone was lying. The fact that she wasn't eased him, taming his instinct to survive and stopping him from viewing her as a threat. She closed in, ignoring the grumbling growls of her mate, and he felt coolness on his wrist and then he was on his feet so quickly the room decided to spin the other way.

Her grip was firmer than the human's had been, strong and unyielding. Not soft and gentle. Not tender.

Not comforting.

Talon squeezed his eyes shut. "Need rest."

"You'll have it," the mortal's voice gently washed over him, soothing him and making him want to look at her.

He risked it, opening his eyes little by little, afraid that the room would still be spinning and he would vomit or pass out. Neither of those things would particularly paint him in a good light. He wanted her to see him as strong, the male he normally was on a good day, but she was seeing him at his worst.

One hell of an introduction.

"You'll be safe," she whispered as she gazed up at him. "I swear it."

He believed her. He would be safe with her. Every instinct he possessed screamed at him to stay with her, that she was the only place where he would ever truly be safe.

Where he would ever truly belong.

She had seen him at his worst, and she looked at him with eyes that held compassion, and a flare of desire. When she saw him at his best, as the warrior he was and the powerful male he had been moulded into by his family, how would she look at him then?

Would she want him as fiercely as he needed her?

"The journey might be rough." Iolanthe grabbed his arm, and tossed a smile at the jaguar. "Be right back."

Before Talon could ask what she was going to do, she had caught hold of the human's arm too and darkness swallowed them all, cold and clinging.

Like Death's embrace.

And all he could think about was that he didn't want to die.

Not because he wanted to avenge someone, or because he wanted to make Archangel pay, or even because he wanted to free the others and return to his pride.

No.

He didn't want to die because he wanted to see her again.

His fated one.

CHAPTER 4

Tiger hit the floor.

Hard.

Sherry looked down at him as she stepped back from Iolanthe, unsurprised by the fact he was out cold. She felt dizzy enough herself and she was at full strength. Her living room wobbled around the edges of her vision, the cream walls blending with her dark violet couch and the oak cabinets and TV stand into a blur of colour.

She eased down into a crouch beside him and pressed her palm to his forehead. What the hell was she doing? It wasn't as if she knew what temperature a tiger shifter normally ran at. She didn't know anything about his species.

She barely knew anything about jaguars and snow leopards, and she had been working with those for years.

But then, other than a few scrapes from when fights broke out in Underworld, neither of them had ever been injured like this.

Neither of them had ever needed her to take care of them.

Sherry looked up at Iolanthe where she towered over her, a stunning vision in black skin-tight armour that moulded to her shapely body and looked designed to get the attention of any males in the vicinity rather than protect the wearer of it.

Apparently, it was designed for the men in her species, and as far as Iolanthe knew, she was the only woman in possession of a set of armour.

She couldn't quite figure out why Iolanthe had chosen to wear it to teleport the tiger to her apartment. It wasn't as if the guy was a threat to Iolanthe, not in his current condition anyway.

Unless Kyter had wanted his beloved covered from neck to toe so the tiger couldn't see any skin. Which was stupid. Because the armour just made Iolanthe look as if someone had painted her naked body black.

But then, the workings of a male cat shifter's mind were often dumb, especially when it came to their women.

Kyter had done enough stupid things in the months since he and Iolanthe had got together, everything from trying to stop his mate from doing her work as a treasure hunter to attempting to hide all her weapons so she couldn't get into any fights, and therefore in his eyes would be absolutely safe from harm.

Which worked for about five seconds before Iolanthe got into a fight and tried to teleport her weapons to her only to find herself cut off from them.

It seemed her boss still hadn't learned that he couldn't stop Iolanthe from doing what she wanted and was just going to have to accept that he had a mate who was strong, and fiercely independent.

Sherry blamed cat shifter society for his behaviour. From what she could tell, women of that world were meant to be all docile and gentle, and in need of a big man to protect them.

She looked back at Tiger.

Was his world like that? Did he expect her to faint at the sight of blood or swoon if someone fought in front of her and cower in fear, waiting for a big man to save her?

Like hell. Life had moulded her into a fighter. If her history with her father hadn't made her strong, then the year she had spent on the streets before Kyter had taken her in certainly had.

And then Kyter had done his best to make her stronger still, paying for lessons in every damned martial art known to man.

Odd how he wanted her to know how to fight and defend herself, had equipped her with the knowledge and weapons to do just that, but he couldn't bring himself to let Iolanthe do the same thing.

Maybe it was one rule for the humans and another for beautiful immortal fae in his eyes.

Or maybe it was because he viewed her as a little sister, and Iolanthe was his mate, and therefore infinitely more precious to him.

Irreplaceable.

How did it feel to be that way to someone?

She considered asking Iolanthe and then immediately scrubbed that idea. She didn't walk in her world. There was no special fated one for her, a one-in-the-world person who had been made just for her. She was just a human, and all that awaited her in life was a string of attempts at love, most of which would fail horribly, and the rest would only fail.

Love was painful and messy.

Life was easier without it.

She had seen that for herself.

She had lived it.

Iolanthe stooped and grabbed the tiger as if he weighed nothing, scooping him up into her arms. It looked ridiculous as the slender elf carried the huge hulking man across the room to the door to the bedroom.

"In here?" Iolanthe glanced over her shoulder at her.

She nodded and got to her feet, and stifled a yawn as she walked across her apartment, kicking her trainers off as she went and leaving them in the middle of the wooden floor. Iolanthe paused again at the side of the double bed.

"You might want to protect the sheets. He's going to make an unholy mess of things otherwise."

True.

Sure, his blood would blend with the burgundy colour of her sheets, and she could wash it out of them, but it would soak through and stain her mattress. She couldn't afford a new mattress and she was damned if she was sleeping on a bloodstained one.

She opened the cupboard set into the wall near the door to her bedroom and took down a stack of towels of all different colours, and went into the bedroom, passing Iolanthe where she stood looking as if the half-dead man in her arms was as light as a feather and no bother at all.

Sherry laid the towels on the bed, four layers deep and hopefully thick enough to soak up any remaining blood before it reached the mattress.

The moment she stepped back, Iolanthe dumped Tiger on them, dusted off her hands and turned away. "He's all yours."

"Gee, thanks." Sherry looked him over, at all the blood on him and the wounds that littered his chest and arms. Some of them looked like burns. She carefully moved his left arm away from his stomach and grimaced at the deep gash across it. Panic clamped icy hands around her heart and she swiftly turned to face Iolanthe. "Wait."

The beautiful elf looked back at her, her dark hair shimmering with blue as it caught the light coming in from the living room.

"I... haven't a damn clue what I'm doing." Her shoulders slumped as she admitted that, some of the tension that had been building inside her since offering to take care of him and keep him safe from Archangel washing away. It felt good to stand up and scream that she was in unknown waters and had zero knowledge of how to traverse them.

Iolanthe casually rolled her shoulders. "Just clean the blood off and patch him up."

"That's it?" She felt stupid for asking now. "Like a human?"

Iolanthe laughed.

"What were you expecting? Some elaborate ritual or special medicine? He'll heal quicker than a human if that makes it more magical for you... but really... shifters aren't that different to you. Even elves just get patched up with bandages when injured... unless they are twisted bastards that enjoy immense pain." She shuddered, her pretty face draining of colour and her violet eyes telling Sherry she didn't want to know. "I'd better go. Kyter will be having cubs. You know what he's like if I'm near another male. Will you be alright?"

Why did everyone keep asking her that?

She wasn't weak or liable to break. She was strong enough to deal with this stranger and take care of herself.

"Of course." She wished there had been more conviction behind those two words, the amount she had meant to put into them.

They had come out unsteady though, laced with nerves and doubt. Iolanthe lingered a moment, studying her closely, and then disappeared, leaving a shimmering patch of air behind her that soon settled.

Sherry looked at the shifter in her bed.

She would be alright.

She would.

Her nerves picked up, kicking into high gear as the apartment fell silent save the sound of her breathing, and it dawned on her that she was alone with him again.

Alone with a shifter who looked even bigger now that he was in her double bed.

A sigh escaped her before she could bite it back.

He was gorgeous.

Breathtaking.

Not just his face either, which was a little rugged but sublimely masculine and alluring even with the long wild black hair and thick beard, and his eyes closed, hiding those striking amber irises from her.

Every inch of him was honed, packed with muscle born of physical labour and not hours in the gym.

She could almost feel how powerful he was just by looking at him, felt bone-deep aware of his strength and prowess as she stood sentinel over him, and felt drawn to him in a way she had never experienced before.

He lit up every inch of her, stirred her desire and sparked her soul, woke her heart and rattled her so hard she wasn't sure what the hell she was doing.

She could only stare at him, could only inch towards him and be closer to him, but even when her knees hit the edge of the mattress she wasn't close enough to satisfy the need he had triggered in her the first time she had looked into his eyes.

She needed to be closer still.

What was he doing to her?

She wanted to blame the fact she hadn't been with a man in a long time, and he was one hell of a fine specimen of one, but part of her was too aware that it ran deeper than that.

That she felt drawn to him because she felt strangely connected to him.

Shit, she was in over her head.

She tried to look at him objectively, checking him from head to toe, but that lasted all of a second before she was bewitched by the sight of him again, by the sheer size of him and how damned alluring that body of his was even when it was covered in blood.

He was everything male and it spoke to her feminine side.

Honed. Powerful. Incredible.

And covered in blood.

Sherry forced herself to focus on that slightly enormous fact.

She had brought him here to tend to his wounds, not gawp at him.

And definitely not to do anything with him.

She looked over his injuries again, her desire fading and a seed of anger blooming inside her, entwined with pity as she lifted her eyes back to his face and stared at him. How long had he been held by Archangel? If he had been clean shaven when they had taken him, it must have been weeks since they had captured him. She wasn't sure how quickly men's facial hair grew, but his beard was several inches long.

He had reacted so violently when Kyter had threatened to send him back to Archangel.

His eyes had held such fear.

She was beginning to believe he was innocent and had done nothing to deserve what Archangel had done to him.

They had hurt him, both physically and mentally, had come close to breaking him if his behaviour at Underworld was anything to go by, and now it was down to her to piece him back together and make him strong again.

She could do this.

She dragged herself away to the bathroom adjoining her bedroom and flicked the light on. She opened the tall white cupboard in the corner beside the pedestal basin and grabbed some cotton balls, a hand towel, bandages and antiseptic, as well as every half-full box of sticking plasters in her collection, and went back into her bedroom.

Tiger moaned and his face scrunched up, flashing canines through his beard at the ceiling before he settled again.

She should have asked him his name when he had been conscious, but he had been in so much pain, and not only physically. There was emotional pain there too. She could recognise it in him, because she had been so familiar with it herself during her upbringing. It was only after Kyter had taken her in that the pain had finally released her and she had been able to mend.

What emotional pain plagued the tiger?

She wanted to know.

She wanted to help him overcome it.

And that meant healing him.

She set everything down on the low cabinet beside the bed, turned on the lamp that stood on it, and then shoved all her clothes off the wooden chair in the corner and dragged it over to his side.

Sherry worked in silence, cleaning the blood off him and then applying antiseptic to the smaller wounds that littered his broad chest and stomach. She kept herself detached from what she was doing, viewing just a small section of him at a time so he didn't distract her from her task with wicked thoughts.

The smaller wounds she left uncovered. The ones that looked as if they needed protection, she covered with a combination of sticking plasters and bandages.

She reached the gash on his stomach and stilled.

It was long, and deep. It looked as if someone had run a knife across him from his left hip to his navel.

What the hell had happened to him?

Was Archangel really responsible for all his wounds?

She grabbed the antiseptic again and set to work, and as she cleaned around the wound, anger began to grow inside her, small at first but rapidly filling the space behind her breasts with fire that spread, until she was dabbing fiercely at the wound, thoughts of setting Archangel to rights whirling around her mind. She was going to find them, and she was going to make them pay for doing such despicable things to Tiger, and to all the other innocents they had apparently captured for the sake of torturing them.

They might not be human, but they weren't so different to them.

They laughed, they loved, they lived in the same way as humans did.

None of them deserved to be treated like laboratory rats.

Sherry pressed the soaked cotton wool ball against the top of the wound on his side, maybe a little too hard.

Tiger growled and tensed, and she stiffened, holding her breath and waiting for him to lash out at her. A low snarl echoed through the room and vibrated through her, strained and gravelly.

She gently laid her hand on his hip, just above the wound, and looked at his face. "Shh, Tiger. Sorry I hurt you."

He settled, his handsome face going lax again and his big body relaxing beneath her touch. His firm lips parted and he exhaled slowly, almost a sigh.

Sherry petted his side, stroking her fingers up and down his warm golden skin, giving him time to fall back asleep before she continued her work. Her touch calmed him, and it calmed her too, the action of caressing him releasing the hold her anger had on her and allowing it to fade again.

"Remind me to get your name when you wake up," she whispered, leaned over to her right and smoothed her fingers across his brow, clearing rogue strands of his wild inky hair from it. "Can't keep calling you Tiger all the time."

He sighed again in his sleep.

She smiled, feathered her fingers down his cheekbones and through the thick mass of beard to his square jaw, and then off him. Hadn't she said she wasn't going to do this? She closed her eyes and sighed to herself, feeling the ground beneath her tremble and quake, on the verge of giving way.

She couldn't fall.

Not for a shifter.

Not for anyone.

Sherry went back to her work, gently easing the two sides of the wound together and then using plasters like stitches to hold them closed so they could fuse and heal. Hopefully it would work. She didn't have anything to stitch him with, or the skills to do such a thing even if she did. When she had covered the length of the wound with plasters, she placed a long folded strip of bandage over it and then stuck it down with more plasters, using them like tape.

It would have to do.

She stifled a yawn and glanced at the clock on her bedside table. Almost five in the morning. She should have been asleep hours ago. It was Sunday now, her one day off in the week, but she had come through the two busiest days for the club, long ones that had left her drained and badly in need of sleep.

She just wanted to crash, but there was a big tiger in her bed.

A tiger who needed her awake and alert, ready to aid him if he needed it.

She was going to need coffee if she was going to stay awake until he came around, keeping an eye on him while he rested and recovered. She couldn't even risk napping. He might react violently if he woke in a strange place. She wanted to be there so he would see a familiar face and would know he was safe.

Sherry tidied everything away in the bathroom and then came back to him, took hold of his left hand and checked his pulse. It was quicker than her own, but then he wasn't human. It could be normal for him.

She gazed down at his large hand, and canted her head, studying the black ink that started at his wrist. It rose in curling lines up his forearm, and formed a tribal design that was almost floral too. She frowned as her gaze caught on something and leaned closer. A tiny bird sat on a swirl that came out from the main design. Another caught her eye higher up, near his elbow. Leaves joined the stunning artwork there, and the tattoo became twisting branches that contained a multitude of animals, all of them hidden amidst the design. She spotted a small rodent-like mammal, and even a deer. There was a whole forest of animals concealed in the leaves and vines on his biceps and shoulder.

From there, the ink spread over his chest in swirling branches and leaves, and hidden among the vines in the centre of his left pectoral, she found a tiger staring back at her.

Sherry brushed her fingers over the ink, captured by the beauty of it.

Whoever had done it, had talent. A pang of envy ran through her, jealousy born of the fact she had never quite found the courage to get a tattoo of her own, even though she wanted one. If someone had offered to do such beautiful work on her, maybe she would have been brave enough to take them up on it.

His ink told a story. She could feel it was personal to him, that it represented his world, and who he was inside.

A beautiful tiger.

She lifted her eyes to his face, and caught a flash of the amber and black fur that had rippled over his chest and arms when he had been fighting Kyter.

What would he look like if he shifted?

She had seen Kyter in his jaguar form a few times, when he couldn't hold it back and needed to shift and take out his aggression in the training room. He had given the plastic barrels hell, biting and clawing them, a huge wild beast that had exuded raw power.

But she hadn't feared him.

Because beneath all the fur, fangs and claws, he was still Kyter.

Would she fear Tiger if he shifted?

Her phone vibrated in her trouser pocket.

She stood and pulled it out, and sighed as she saw the name on the screen.

She swiped her thumb across it as she exited the bedroom and brought the phone up to her ear. "Kyter?"

"I was worried you wouldn't answer."

Sherry sighed again and rolled her eyes. "Did you think the tiger would have eaten me already?"

"This isn't a joke, Sherry. That male is dangerous."

"Dangerously unconscious. Look, I'm fine... and I know you're worried... but really, I'm fine. He's out cold. He barely stirred when I was fixing his wounds." She swapped ears as she turned to glance back into her bedroom at the sleeping tiger. "I don't think he's any danger to me."

"He's more danger to you than you think. He—" Kyter cut himself off, and she frowned at the tiger. He what? What was it about this tiger that had Kyter so wound up? She was about to ask, when he spoke again. "I'm sending Cavanaugh over."

"No." That wasn't going to happen. "My house isn't Cav's territory, and he's pretty chill for a cat shifter, but he's still a guy... and a cat... and it wouldn't exactly be the first time he's lost his shit around another guy shifter."

So it had only happened the once, but it had been brutal and the poor guy on the receiving end of the attack hadn't known what had hit him. Kyter had been forced to close the club and restrain Cavanaugh until he had finally regained control and shifted back from his snow leopard form.

Tiger wasn't strong enough to withstand that sort of attack.

She went into the small kitchen on the other side of the apartment to the bedroom and stuck a fresh filter into her coffee maker and filled it with grounds from the refrigerator. Any second now, Kyter would get his temper back down to a simmer and would bounce back, finding another way to tell her that Tiger was a threat to her and convince her to let Cavanaugh come to protect her.

She didn't need a man to protect her.

She never had.

"Fine," Kyter grumbled.

Not quite what she had expected. It wasn't like her boss to lie down so easily and roll over. Normally it took at least three rounds of arguing her point before he gave up.

"But you have to call me the second he wakes up, got it?" Kyter's voice was little more than a rough growl, and it struck her just how deeply he cared about her, and just how worried he was that she was alone with a strange shifter.

Guilt squirmed in her gut, making her feel queasy.

She wanted to apologise for how she had insisted she take care of Tiger, wanted to reassure him that she would be alright and he didn't have to worry, even though she knew it wouldn't stop him, but in the end she settled for saying, "I will."

"Io will be there like a shot. We're just a phone call away. Keep it close and call if you need us." The note of worry in his voice touched her and she smiled into the phone.

"Softie."

He snorted. "Just don't want to see my years of hard work turning you into the best bartender we have go down the drain because some dumb tiger got it into his head to eat you and you were too stubborn to admit you were wrong about him."

A laugh bubbled from her lips. "He might surprise you."

"Yeah… I think he might have already done that. Be careful."

The line went dead.

Her smile fell and she brought the phone away from her ear and frowned at it. What the hell had he meant by that?

She looked through the kitchen door towards the bedroom. What was it about this tiger that had Kyter so on edge?

The need to stay awake grew stronger, a trickle of fear about being alone with the tiger sliding down her spine, and she filled the coffee maker with water and turned it on. She played with her phone while it brewed, leaning with her backside against the fake granite kitchen counter.

Surfing the net passed thirty minutes, and watching TV on the couch with a freshly brewed cup of coffee saw another hour fly past. Sunlight streamed through the window of her living room to her left by the time her stomach growled in protest. She left the violet couch, looked down at herself and huffed.

Maybe she should have changed.

Muddy red splotches covered her white shirt. His blood. He had been so worried about getting it on her. She looked into the bedroom and drifted towards it.

Towards him.

He slept soundly on one side of her bed, his lips parted and chest rising and falling on his shallow breaths. He had moved at some point, because his hands rested on his bare stomach, his left one covering the bandaged wound, the fingers slightly drawn so they gathered the material. Had it comforted him to feel the wound bound now?

No longer bleeding?

She couldn't imagine how terrifying it would be to have such a vicious injury, to feel life slipping from you like that.

Or how strong he had to be to keep going, and not give up.

She slipped quietly into the room, found a pair of dark grey lounge pants in the cream chest of drawers near the bathroom door, and pulled out a white camisole. She checked him again, and then went into the white and cream bathroom and changed her clothes, tossing her dirty white shirt, black slacks, and underwear on the floor in the corner near the shower cubicle.

She used a sponge to wipe off the blood on her stomach and then tugged on her white camisole and grey loose soft pants.

Shit, it felt good to be in fresh clean clothes.

She wanted a shower, but no way she was going to risk it. She wasn't sure how long Tiger would be out and if he woke when she was naked, he might view it as an invitation.

Sherry pocketed her phone, slipped back into the bedroom and tiptoed through it. When she hit the wooden living room floor, she padded across it to the oak table wedged between the TV and the couch, grabbed her cup and headed for the kitchen.

Coffee.

She needed more.

A yawn escaped her as she poured another cup, and grabbed a cereal bar from the cupboard above the machine. Her phone buzzed against her thigh. She sighed, pulled it out and checked it. Kyter again. At least he was only messaging her this time.

She fired back a reply that the tiger still hadn't eaten her, and went back to the couch.

Time trickled past as she watched TV and fiddled around on the internet, checking Facebook and then adding around a thousand things to her wish lists on several shopping websites, and answered a million more texts from Kyter, and one from Cavanaugh the one time she took more than a minute to reply to Kyter. That one had told her that Kyter was driving him mad and to text him back ASAP.

She ate lunch sometime in the early afternoon, and the coffee started to lose its effect a few hours later. She yawned and blinked hard as her eyes watered, and sleep beckoned.

She had to stay awake.

Sherry rubbed her eyes, stood and walked around the couch and to the window. She lifted the sash, breathed in the cool city air, gazed at the faint stars and then watched people coming and going along the street below. It kept her awake for all of five minutes before sleep washed over her again, making her eyelids heavy.

Another coffee might help.

Probably wouldn't, but it was worth a shot.

She closed the window.

Tiger roared.

Cold washed through her followed by a flash of heat, and a delicious sort of trembling between her thighs that lasted only a second before fear chased it away when Tiger started thrashing around, kicking at the covers and clawing at her sheets.

She rushed into her bedroom and grabbed his shoulders, and pushed down with all of her weight and strength, trying to restrain him so he didn't reopen his wounds.

He bucked and snarled, and fought her, easily dislodging her and sending her sprawling on her backside on the hard floor. Damn, that was going to bruise. She leaped to her feet and grabbed him again, unwilling to give up even when it was clear he was too strong for her to hold down. His breathing quickened, his struggle escalating until she was forced to get onto the bed and straddle him to hold him down.

He loosed a harrowing whimper that chilled her blood and made her heart bleed for him, and then roared.

"Jayna!"

Tiger launched forwards, his head connected hard with the side of hers, and the room danced and spun around her. Lightning arced over her skull and white stars burst and died before her eyes.

She groaned and slumped onto her butt on his knees, clutching her head and fighting the sickening wave of pain that rolled over her.

Tiger suddenly froze right down to his breathing, his amber eyes alert and wide.

"You okay?" she murmured, battling another wave of sickness as he wobbled in her vision.

Shit, he had a hard head.

He nodded.

She managed a smile. "That's g-r-r-r-eat!"

And promptly passed out.

CHAPTER 5

Talon shifted sideways, his eyes locked with the tiger's, circling with it as it stalked him. She bared fangs on a hiss and he bared his own back at her, showing her that he wasn't going to back down. She had to stop this madness.

He had to stop it.

He glanced off to his left, barely taking his eyes off her, not giving her a chance to attack him. They were watching on the other side of all the mirror glass and bars that protected it.

Bastards.

What cocktail of drugs had they given her this time?

They had dragged him to the cage and he had noticed on the way past that her cell in the stark white block had been empty. He had asked them where they had taken her, had demanded to know what they had done to her.

He had been given his answer when they had tossed him into the cage, a huge white room with a thick solid glass divide down the middle of it.

On the other side of that barrier had been the tiger he had been looking for.

But at the same time, it hadn't been her.

She had been brutally attacking the barrels and logs in her cat form, pouncing on anything she spotted and savagely biting and clawing at it. It wasn't like her. He had only known her a short time, but it had been long enough for him to learn she had a gentle soul.

Not a violent one.

Archangel had given her something to awaken her aggressive nature, setting it free and unleashing the primal side of her in the process.

She had lifted her head when she had scented him, and the moment they had raised the barrier, she had attacked him.

He had taken her blows, blocking as many of them as he could, defending and never attacking her, hoping beyond hope that the drug would wear off if he withstood her assault for long enough and she would come to her senses.

"Listen to my voice, Jayna," he murmured softly, coaxing her to come back to him.

She bared huge canines again and launched at him.

Talon caught her and twisted with her, slammed her into the bloodstained floor and tried to pin her. She hissed and snarled, writhed and kicked at him, and he barely reared back in time to avoid her fangs as she snapped at his head.

"Dammit," he barked and fought harder, because he wasn't going to give up on her.

He was going to bring her back.

"Jayna." He wrestled with her, managed to get hold of her thick front legs and stop her from clawing him.

She wasn't listening, was too deep in her animal side to hear and recognise him. It was in control now.

She wriggled her back legs free of his hold and he didn't stand a chance.

Before he could spring away from her, she kicked at his stomach.

He sucked it in and arched backwards, but one claw caught him and he grunted and growled through clenched teeth as it cut through his flesh and fire followed in its wake.

"Fuck!" He shoved off her and staggered backwards, agony rolling through him as he clutched his left side and hot blood pumped over his hand and down his leg, sticking his standard-issue black cotton trousers to his thigh. "Jayna, stop this!"

Because it wasn't like her. It wasn't her.

And if she didn't stop soon, he wasn't sure he would be able to bring her back. The more she hurt him, the stronger the hold her tiger side had on her would become, until she wouldn't want to come back.

He had to stop her, before her mind cracked.

He eyed her warily as she rolled onto her paws and paced away from him, and stopped near the mirrored window. Sickness washed through him again when she paused to lick at wounds on her own belly, cleaning blood away from her soft pale golden fur.

If the bastards hadn't cracked her mind already.

She'd had new wounds tonight, low on her stomach.

The thought they might have been probing around down there, hurting her body and her mind with their twisted study of her, sickened him.

He would never forgive himself if anything happened to her.

Jayna suddenly sprang at the bars protecting the window.

The sizzle of electricity filled the room together with the stench of burning flesh as the defence system built into them fired. It didn't stop Jayna from biting at the bars and clawing them.

"No." He was across the room in the blink of an eye and hauling her off the bars and shoving her away.

She flashed her fangs on a growl and tried to pass him, but he countered her every move, blocking her way to the bars.

Jayna roared and launched straight at him, tackling him to the ground. He screamed as she sank her fangs into his right side, a bite meant to weaken him, and kicked off. He tried to grab her, but he was too slow to stop her.

By the time he had rolled onto his front, she was at the bars again, attacking them despite the charge they were pumping into her. She whimpered and hissed, drew back and attacked again, unrelenting in her assault.

"Stop," he croaked but she ignored him and kept biting the bars, clawing and scratching at them with her front paws.

The scent of burning flesh and singeing fur swamped him and he choked back a cry as he pushed onto his feet and grabbed her tail, tugged hard on it and pulled her away from the bars.

She whimpered as she convulsed violently on the floor, and her fur rippled and washed away, leaving pink skin behind.

Jayna curled up and held herself, tears streaking her face as she shook. Blood covered her belly and thighs, and splattered across her breasts and shoulders. It streaked her face and surrounded her mouth.

"Jayna," he whispered and she looked at him, her amber eyes dull and overflowing with sorrow and pain.

Talon shook his head and held his hand out to her.

She screamed like a banshee and in a lightning fast move was on her feet and clutching the bars with her hands again. Her body quaked as electricity poured through it and she threw her head back and shrieked.

He grabbed her around the waist and hauled her away from them. She growled and kicked at his legs, her hands clawing at his arms where he wrapped them around her waist. He locked them tight. Refused to let her go.

The blood on her made it hard to keep his grip on her though, and she slid down his body, her cries of pain haunting his ears as he struggled to keep hold of her and awareness crept in, cold and numbing.

He knew what she wanted to do.

He couldn't let it happen. He would never forgive himself if anything happened to her. He had vowed to protect her.

"Don't," he whispered, broken and hoarse, silently pleading her to listen to him.

She was still a moment.

And then she pressed her left foot into his thigh, twisted in his arms and shoved her hands against his chest, pushing free of his grip. He staggered back a step and then sprang forwards, grabbed her arm and pulled her back to him. She grunted as she slammed into his bare chest and he growled as she clawed and bit him, and then threw his head back and cried out as she shoved her fingers into the wound on his side and tore at it.

He stumbled backwards as she kicked off again, and clutched his side. Warm blood rolled from between his fingers and the edges of his vision went dark. Dammit.

No.

Jayna stopped and stood before him, her face soft, amber eyes shining at him even though there was so much pain in her.

Talon reached his right hand out to her.

A flash of regret crossed her face.

"Don't do this," he pleaded. "Don't."

She pivoted on her heel and launched at the bars, grabbed hold of them and didn't let go this time.

His stomach sank, his heart breaking as he realised he couldn't stop her.

As he realised she wanted death.

Archangel had already broken her—mind, body and soul.

He had failed.

"No," he whispered, and moved a step towards her.

She hissed at him, her eyes begging him to let her do this.

For him.

It was the way of their kind, but that didn't mean he was alright with it. It was a stupid tradition. The weaker protecting the stronger.

He couldn't bear it.

He didn't want her to sacrifice herself so he could live.

She screamed and fur rippled over her naked body, but she kept holding the bars, somehow finding the strength and the courage to not let go.

Talon couldn't watch.

He didn't deserve this.

His pride would never forgive him for failing her.

His family would never forgive him.

And he would never forgive himself.

He would never forgive Archangel.

She collapsed and he rushed to her, gathered her limp form into his arms and cleared the black hair from her face. She breathed shallowly, panted gasps that rasped in his ears and tore at his heart. He should have stopped her. Her eyelids fluttered and then lifted, and she looked up at him, the gentle and beautiful female he had known her to be.

A smile tilted her lips.

Her eyes dulled and her breath left her on a soft sigh, and she sank in his arms.

Slipped through his hands and into the eternal forest where her ancestors waited for her.

Talon threw his head back and roared.

"Jayna!"

CHAPTER 6

Pain splintered into a thousand fault lines over Talon's skull as it connected hard with something.

A something that loosed a muffled grunt and moved on his lap, swaying to one side and muttering to herself.

His breathing stilled, hammering heart slowing as he grew painfully aware of the slender weight on his lap, pressing down on his thighs, and the warmth of her that soaked through the thin sheets covering his lower half.

He opened his eyes and stared into the female's blue ones, his pain forgotten together with his nightmare as he drowned in their infinite skies.

Gods, she was as beautiful as he remembered, and apparently not a dream.

He gave her a quick once over.

Although, she had been dressed differently in the dream that had preceded his nightmare replay of the last day, wearing a provocative little black slip rather than homely grey light cotton trousers and a tight fitting white strappy top.

"You okay?" she whispered, her soft voice curling around him, chasing away the last remnants of his nightmare and freeing him of its hold.

He nodded dumbly, still not quite over the fact he had come around to find her straddling him.

She smiled. "That's g-r-r-r-eat!"

Before he could pick her up on the fact he was no cartoon tiger on the carton of a breakfast food, she collapsed into his chest, her cheek smashing against his right pectoral.

Icy tendrils snaked through him and he quickly leaned back to check on her.

Her button nose wrinkled and she moaned, smacked her lips together and settled against his chest, rubbing her cheek against it as if she was a damned cat too.

The fear building in his veins washed away.

She was just sleeping.

Although the bang to the head he had given her had probably helped her fall into sleep's waiting embrace.

He took in his cookie cutter surroundings, with its magnolia walls and wooden furniture that made it look as if she had purchased the cover of a home style magazine. On the bedside table, an alarm clock revealed the hour was late, close to eleven at night, meaning she had been awake all day watching over him.

It was little wonder she was fast asleep now.

Talon returned his gaze to her and studied her in silence, absorbing how beautiful she appeared in sleep, her face soft with it and rosy lips parted. Her warm breath skated across his chest, her skin heating his, and he didn't want to move.

Not because he might wake her.

He just didn't want to end this, whatever this was.

His heart thumped hard, as if the stupid thing wanted to jump right out of his body and into her arms.

Talon sighed and ghosted his left hand over her bare arm, down from her shoulder to her hand, and let his fingers brush over hers. They froze there. What the fuck was he doing?

This would only end in him getting his heart broken.

But he couldn't help himself.

She was meant to be his, so why couldn't he have her?

That quiet persistent voice at the back of his mind warned that he knew why.

It was too dangerous.

But still he couldn't stop himself.

He preened her golden hair from her face, stroked his fingers down the sleek length of her ponytail, and lifted it towards his nose. He inhaled deeply, drawing her scent of vanilla and honey down into him, so it mingled and became part of him, and imprinted onto his memory.

Gods, she was beautiful.

Maybe even more so as she slept in his arms, because her guard was down and she was allowing him to be near to her when she was vulnerable, relying on him to protect her and trusting him not to hurt her.

He pressed a kiss to her hair and let it slip from his fingers. "Thank you."

For watching over him. For patching him up. For giving him sanctuary.

For being so unguarded around him.

Not many people in this world would help a stranger as she had, or allow them into her home and take care of them, or trust them so easily and have faith in them.

He looked her over again. Small, but fierce. Brave. Strong.

She reminded him of Jayna.

Talon squeezed his eyes shut, wishing he could shut out the pain as easily.

He opened his eyes and looked down at the female resting against his chest, forced himself to see how different she was to Jayna. He was just hurting from reliving what had happened in vivid detail, seeing similarities between them that weren't really there because he wanted to cling to the idea Jayna wasn't gone, and that he wasn't going to be in the deepest sort of shit when he got back to the pride.

This human was small, but fierce. Brave. Strong.

Jayna had been more gentle, delicate in a way that had grated at times, subservient to the end. She had sacrificed herself so he could have a shot at living, obeying the rules and traditions of their kind.

Something told him that the woman in his arms would tell him to go to Hell if he told her to end her life so he could go on living because he was stronger than her, better able to survive and go on to expand their pride. She would laugh if he told her what an honour it was, and that as a female she was meant to do as she was told.

Gods, she would be right to do that too.

Maybe he had believed in traditions when he had been a kid, starry-eyed and awed by everything his parents and teachers had told him, had hammered into his tiny skull until he had thought tigers were the best species in the world and everyone else was below them, because they didn't have such wonderful, and powerful traditions.

He had thought those traditions noble once.

Now they just seemed backwards and stupid, dreamed up by males in a position of power who didn't want to die, so they decreed that the weak should sacrifice themselves for the sake of the strong if it ever came down to it.

Stupid.

Talon brushed her golden hair behind her shoulder and barely resisted teasing the nape of her neck with his fingertips. His heart thudded hard, drumming against her cheek, beating for her.

It was the duty of the strong to protect the weak.

It was his duty to fight until he had no more fight left in him, and then keep going, until he was spent.

Until he could die with honour, because he had done his best.

He didn't want people sacrificing themselves for him. He wanted to be the one who did that for others, wanted to use his strength to shield others and save them.

The entire pride would laugh at him if they heard that.

Or be horrified.

He didn't give a fuck though. The gods had made him strong, a warrior, and he would use that strength for the sake of others.

He wouldn't fail anyone again. If Jayna's sacrifice had done anything for him, it had awoken him to his true purpose. He had allowed her to die, and he would never allow that to happen to another, not when he had the power left in his body to protect them.

His tiger side settled again, contented by the feel of the human in his arms and his resolve to be true to his nature and screw the rules.

He would start by heading back to Archangel. His stomach twisted at the thought of dishonouring Jayna's sacrifice by returning there and placing himself in danger again, but some part of his soul whispered that she would understand. He would use her sacrifice to save not only himself.

He would save the others too.

He carefully eased the human down onto the bed and slipped out from under her. Gods, that was one of the hardest things he had ever done. He wanted to stay close to her, but he needed to keep his distance too.

It was for the best.

He rolled from the bed and groaned as he stretched and the wound above his left hip burned. Dammit. A little longer. He just needed to be patient a little longer and then he would be strong enough.

Talon looked back over his shoulder at the sleeping female and slowly turned towards her. Her nose wrinkled again and then she sighed softly. He cleared the towels she had spread across the mattress, hoping to fuck that he hadn't bled everywhere, and grimaced when he noticed the slashes in her dark crimson bedclothes.

Oops.

He would have to buy her new ones.

Inside he purred at that, at the thought he could see her again, could watch her face light up when he presented her with a gift.

Maybe she would even throw herself into his arms.

He huffed, tamped down that stupid desire, and pressed one knee into the mattress and leaned over the bed. He carefully scooped her up into his arms, set her down in the middle of the bed, and covered her.

She burrowed into the pillows, rubbing her face against the one he had been sleeping on.

The one covered with his scent.

Talon groaned, and it became a low growl as he thought about how he wanted her covered with his scent. He wanted every male shifter who came near her to smell him on her.

To know that she was his.

"Shit," he muttered and raked a hand over his black hair.

He needed to get these urges under control before he did something reckless and foolish, something that might place his entire pride in danger.

Talon backed off one step and then another, forcing himself away from the temptation sleeping before him. He had to do something to get his mind off her.

He looked down at his body, at the bandages that littered it, and smiled. Enthusiastic about her work? There was no way any of the wounds he'd had, with the exception of the gash across his stomach, had needed this amount of attention, but he wasn't about to complain. He viewed the myriad of bandages and sticking plasters as a mark of her affection. A purr rumbled in his chest. His female cared about him already.

Talon cleared his throat.

Not his female.

He had to stop thinking like that.

What he really needed to do was get clean, but he couldn't shift. It wasn't the injuries stopping him. It was damned tradition, one he couldn't quite bring himself to break with. The laws of his species required him to remain in his mortal form for the first three nights of grieving. He had barely known Jayna a few months, but she deserved this from him.

So he wouldn't shift and clean himself.

He would do it the mortal way.

Talon spotted the open door to the bathroom and padded across the room to it, rounding the foot of the double bed and diligently keeping his eyes away from the female sleeping in it. He stepped into the bright room and curled his lip at the fact the cookie cutter appearance of her home continued there, in the form of a plain white suite, cream walls and pale tiles.

Still, he wasn't going to complain.

It had a shower, a gift from the gods themselves.

He had hated the days of wooden tubs and boiling water over a fire. By the time the tub had been filled, the damned water had always been tepid at best.

Talon stripped off his loose black cotton trousers and kicked them onto the pile of her clothes near the shower cubicle. He didn't bother to close the bathroom door. It wasn't because he wanted her to wake and see him naked. It really wasn't. It was because he wanted to hear if she stirred.

Honestly, it was.

He kept telling himself that as he reached into the double shower and twisted the knob to start the flow of water. When it had reached temperature, he stepped inside and slid the door closed behind him.

And groaned.

Gods, the hot water felt good. He couldn't remember the last time he had been warmed by water rather than chilled to the bone. When was the last time he'd had a shower because he had wanted one?

It was bliss.

A beautiful departure from the pelting with a freezing cold hose that Archangel had delivered every week or so, whenever he got too bloodstained and dirty for them.

Couldn't think about that.

He closed his eyes and ducked his head under the water, pressed his hands to the tiles beyond the jet and stayed there, letting the heat wash over him and carry away those memories. He wasn't there now. He was somewhere quite the opposite to that wretched place.

He was safe.

Thanks to the female sleeping just a few feet from him.

Dammit, what had the jaguar called her?

He recalled him speaking her name, but the pain had been so intense at times that everything had been garbled in his ears, fragmented and distorted. He frowned at his feet, watching the water swirling down the drain.

Shifted his gaze to the plasters and bandages covering him.

He drew his right hand away from the wall and picked at one low on his stomach, trying not to think about how she had put it there, had touched his body and taken care of him. His cock wasn't listening, rose hard and fast to attention, and he groaned as his thoughts took him down dangerous paths, making him imagine her hands on him, her whispered words of reassurance as she tended to him, and how her stunning blue eyes would look filled with desire, longing caused by her touching him, seeing his bare chest and imagining naughty things herself.

Talon palmed his length, shuddered and bit back a low groan as fire shot down his cock to his balls and they tingled.

Fuck.

He dragged his hand away and planted it against the tiles, because he was damned if he was going to jack off in the shower like some damned teen who had no control over his body.

His cock twitched, jerking and getting his attention again.

No.

He ripped another plaster off his chest, grimaced as it tore hairs with it and stung like a bitch. He tackled another, and then a third, using the pain to divert his thoughts away from the female sleeping in the other room and all the wicked things he wanted to do with her.

She was beautiful.

And strong.

Both of heart and of body.

He figured she worked for the jaguar, which explained why she had guts and could handle herself. She was beautiful. *Beautiful.* Damn near bewitching with it. Beauty could be a curse though. Another sticking plaster and bandage combo joined the rest in the shower tray at his feet.

She probably had to deal with her fair share of rowdy males because she was beautiful.

More than beautiful.

Sherry.

He frowned at his feet.

Her name was Sherry.

The jaguar had called her that.

How the hell did a human come to work for a jaguar shifter in a club that reeked of fae, shifters and demons anyway?

He looked over his shoulder at the door to the bedroom.

He wanted to know.

He wanted to know her story.

Because he wanted to know her. He wanted to be closer to her.

That bastard little voice murmured that it was dangerous, that she was mortal.

Why couldn't she have been any other species?

Any other one and he could have given in to the desires building within him, the fierce need that seized him from time to time and tried to overpower him.

The hunger to sink his fangs into that sweet nape of hers and mark her.

If he lost himself in the moment like that with any other species, it wouldn't mean a thing, would be nothing more than rough love play that would bind them as mates.

If he bit Sherry.

Talon shook that tempting thought away, because it was too dangerous to even think about it. For both of them. For his pride. If anyone learned his family's secret, their name would be worth nothing, their banner torn down from the lofty heights of tiger society and trampled into the dirt.

It was never going to happen.

He kept telling himself that as he switched off the shower, stepped out and dried off. He told himself it as he slung a towel around his waist and tied it. Told himself it as he washed his black trousers in the sink and hung them to dry over the heated towel rail. Told himself it as he used her razor and a pair of scissors to shave his beard and trim his hair, making himself more presentable—for her.

Kept telling himself it but he couldn't seem to drum it into his head or his heart, and he found himself standing beside the bed again, watching her as she slept.

Sherry was his.

Talon knew that in his blood, had felt it the second he had set eyes on her.

He could claim her, could do it in secret and keep her away from the pride, and no one would discover his family's secret. She could be his. He would claim her.

He stilled.

Pushed away from that tempting thought as he looked at her where she slept soundly, unaware of his thoughts, of what he wanted to do to her.

Archangel had taken away his free will, had forced him into their world of pain and terror.

He couldn't take away her right to choose.

He couldn't be like them.

Maybe he would have once, would have pursued her until she had given in to him, until she had given him what he wanted even if it hadn't been what she truly desired.

He chuckled at that, but it was mirthless and cold.

Archangel had beaten the shit out of him, tortured and tried to break him, all in an effort to learn about him. Turned out they were the ones who had taught him something.

They had taught him that free will was precious, and that everyone should have a choice, even if their decision was one that he didn't want.

All he could do was show Sherry what he could be for her, that he would do all in his power to protect and cherish her if she gave him a chance, and he would place her on a pedestal and give her everything she desired if she only asked it of him.

If she stepped into his world.

That day was a long way off though.

He knew a little about humans and how they worked, and he was going to have to start with the basics and be patient, even when it went against his nature, when he was already screaming with need of her, need to have her and make her his mate.

He blew out his breath.

The basics.

Getting to know her.

Letting her know him.

Or at least some of him. He needed to keep some things from her, because he was a betting male and he bet she knew a few things about shifters.

He stifled a yawn and followed the smell of stale coffee into the living room and through it to the small kitchen. He was beat, needed at least another thirty to forty hours of sleep to fully heal, or maybe he just wanted to sleep through the mourning period.

With Sherry.

He couldn't sleep though, so he poured the remnants of the coffee jug into a mug and drank it down. Sleeping meant letting the nightmares back in, and they only made him feel more tired. He wouldn't find the rest he needed if he slept now.

There was another reason he needed to stay awake too.

He found the filters and the coffee grounds, and set about brewing a fresh pot.

He needed to repay Sherry by protecting her while she slept.

He wasn't convinced that Archangel wouldn't find him here, and he was damned if they were going to catch him napping.

He wouldn't let Archangel do to her what they had done to Jayna.

When there was enough coffee in the bottom of the jug, he poured himself another mug. Never had been patient. It was going to be a tough journey to winning Sherry over if he couldn't learn to have a little patience though. Good things came to those who waited.

He paused on the threshold of the living room.

When had he resolved to risk everything for her?

It hit him that he had made that decision the moment he had set eyes on her and all the struggle and doubts since then had been redundant, all the fear of exposing his family and the noble desire to place them before himself and let Sherry go had been a lie.

Because he wanted her.

Talon slumped onto the dark purple couch, picked up the remote from the wooden coffee table and flicked channels. He pulled down a deep breath, catching her scent of honey and vanilla among the aroma of the coffee in his hand, and closed his eyes, savouring it.

He wanted her.

But would she want him if she knew the truth about him?

CHAPTER 7

Sherry had been having the most delicious dream about a black-haired warrior and a desert island somewhere in the tropics. He had been a vision as he had waded out of crystal turquoise waters towards her where she sat on white sands, water rolling down his bare ripped body.

Looking for all the world like some decadent sea god.

She rubbed sleep from her eyes and rested her hand across her face, a contented sigh slipping from her lips as she held on to the dream, wanting to experience it a little longer.

Bliss.

Sheer Heaven.

Or it would have been if she hadn't woken just when it had been getting *really* good.

She shivered, warmed from head to toe from the memory of the fantasy and how his hands had felt as they had traversed her, and how very wickedly good his skilled tongue had felt when he had delved between her thighs.

A moan bubbled up her throat.

She quickly swallowed it down when the sound coming from the other room suddenly changed from a low murmured conversation to a blasting rock anthem.

She wasn't alone.

Awareness hit her like a bucket of icy water, swiftly followed by a flash of wildfire that burned up her blood as she remembered she hadn't come home all by herself last night.

Tiger had come with her.

She shot onto her knees in the middle of the double bed and stared into the other room.

The delicious black-haired warrior was sitting on her plum couch.

Her hands darted to her head, felt the mass of bed hair, and she grimaced. Damn. She hurried from the bed, her legs tangling in the burgundy sheets and almost sending her sprawling face first onto the hard floor. She saved herself at the last second, kicking her foot free, and hopped into the bathroom as she fought for balance.

It took her record time to fix her appearance, brushing her hair and tying it in a neat ponytail. When she went to tackle her teeth, her eyes widened, her right hand freezing on her toothbrush in the beige faux-stone pot. Black hairs covered the white porcelain sink. She glanced over her right shoulder, her eyebrows shooting up when she spotted the dressings left all over the shower tray.

He had used her shower?

He had shaved?

A tremor went through her, a ripple of heat that stirred naughty thoughts as she tried to imagine how he would look without the beard. The length of the hairs in the sink said it wasn't only his beard he had dealt with—he had cut his hair too.

Hell, he had affected her badly enough when he had been scruffy and unkempt. She didn't want to imagine how deeply he was going to affect her now, wasn't sure she could prepare herself for it, not even if she had all day and all night.

She dealt with her teeth, desperately needing something mundane to focus on as she gathered herself. When she had rinsed her mouth out and cleaned her toothbrush, and it was back in the holder, she sucked down a deep breath to steady her nerves and then walked through the bedroom and into the living room as calmly as she could with her heart jittering around all over the place in her chest.

The second she entered the living room, he looked over the back of the couch at her.

Damn.

Tiger was fine with a capital F.

Gorgeous.

Wild.

His glossy black hair was chopped crudely around the sides, as close to his scalp as he could manage, but left longer on top, a little wavy and wild, and a fine shadow of stubble caressed his square jaw. Damn. His lips were devastating, full and tempting, beckoning her and rousing a fierce need to kiss him.

The black slash of his right eyebrow slowly rose.

Sherry shook herself out of the trance he had put her in just by looking at her.

"You're up... and still here." She smiled at him, and felt stupid for stating the obvious.

She should have said something better, although she wasn't sure what *better* would have been. Damn nerves. So there was a hot guy, a damn hot guy, sitting on her couch staring at her, there was no reason to let it affect her this badly. He was just a guy after all.

For a moment, she felt sure he would smile right back, but his lips didn't quirk and his amber eyes didn't shine. They both remained flat and cold.

"Ready to talk yet, Tony?" she said, a little more cautious now, keeping some distance between them as the mood shifted in the room, taking some of her nerves with it because he clearly wasn't riding the same wavelength as she was, didn't look at all interested in her as he had last night.

Maybe she had surprised him with her sudden appearance, or he was different to the Adonis that had invaded her dreams.

The black slashes of his eyebrows dipped low.

Okay, so he didn't appreciate the Tony tag but she didn't know his name, and calling him Tiger felt too personal.

Too intimate.

He had drawn a line between them, one she had needed because it had shaken the last vestiges of the dream from her, freeing her of its fantasy and reminding her that she had vowed she wasn't going to do this. She wasn't going to think of Tiger in that way.

She really wasn't.

She moved to stand at the end of the couch and frowned at the sight of him. He had removed most of the plasters and bandages she had put over his wounds, leaving only the one that covered the deep gash that cut across his stomach on his left side. He had also washed his black trousers. In the shower? Where he had left all the dirty dressings in the tray like an animal.

Or a man.

He was healing though, and looked healthier already.

He nodded, tipped his head back and sighed, one that stirred wicked heat that licked at her belly and breasts, and roused naughty thoughts despite her attempts to squash them before they could take hold.

His eyes opened a crack and slid towards her as they narrowed.

Sherry moved away, hurrying towards the kitchen, hoping to escape before he could pick her up on the way she reacted to him. Kyter had told her once that shifters were sensitive to scents, could smell when a female wanted them or a male wanted to fight them. Something about pheromones.

She didn't want him scenting things on her.

Not because it would be embarrassing, but because she had the feeling that he was already something to someone else.

Someone called Jayna.

A vicious hiss sounded in her head, her heart spitting at that name with venom.

"Want some coffee?" she said, managing to keep the sharp bite of jealousy out of her voice, and then added as she peered back at him, "Or cereal? I might have a box of Frosties somewhere."

He scowled over at her, and then did something that surprised her.

He laughed.

It was warm, rich, and a little awkward, as if he wasn't used to laughing, or perhaps he had meant it to sound mocking and sarcastic, but it had come out real and surprised him too.

The lack of lines bracketing those kissable lips backed up the feeling she had that he rarely smiled.

Sherry stared at them.

And stared.

Stared.

Lost herself a little in how good they had felt in her dream, against her lips, her throat. Her breasts.

"You're not very funny," he said, a dull edge to his tone.

She blinked herself back to him, caught the look in his amber eyes that said he wanted to pick her up on her spacing out while gazing at his mouth, but he was going to let it slide this time.

"So... coffee, Tony?" It seemed like a good way to hide in the kitchen for a few minutes and get herself back under control.

Something about him made her usual cool and collected circuits go haywire, as if he was overloading her senses and she just couldn't keep control around him. He stirred dangerous impulses, and a tempting little voice that coaxed her into going along with them.

He didn't help when he stood, all delicious muscle bunching and flexing as he twisted towards her, and said, "Talon."

She stared at him, needing a moment to catch up, because she was still doing a slow replay of just how his powerful body moved, how it came alive and screamed of strength, prodded that feminine part of her that reacted to him on a biological level in response.

Male. Strong. Powerful. Perfect breeding material.

Now she was starting to sound like the damn shifters she worked with.

She was more than biology, than nature, and she wasn't going to give into it. She had never been one for lust before, for letting her body control her, and she wasn't going to start now.

"Sorry, Tony?" she muttered, making a valiant attempt to pull her eyes away from the thick ropes of muscle that formed one hell of an impressive eight pack, and the twin slabs that cried out for her to smooth her palms over them, and trace the tattoo that covered the left one.

Maybe even lick it.

He prowled towards her, his body a living symphony as his long legs devoured the small distance between them, and the feel of his eyes on her had her blood rolling from a simmer to a white-hot boil.

"Talon," he husked, too damn sexy sounding for his own good.

Or hers.

He stopped close to her, near enough she could feel the heat coming off him, could smell the lingering scent of her body wash on his skin. Skin she wanted to lick and nip at until he sighed in that way he had while sitting on her couch, all contentment and satisfaction. She started when his fingers brushed her jaw, and didn't resist him as he slowly lifted her chin, bringing her eyes up to meet his.

Stunning.

Gold shone around his wide pupils.

Hunting her?

Kyter and Cavanaugh had taught her to tell when a shifter was on the hunt by the way their eyes changed.

They had also taught her that desire altered them in the same way.

Maybe Tiger wanted her after all.

"My name is Talon," he murmured, as if he had read her thoughts. "And yours is Sherry."

"You remember that?" she said, a little breathless, a hell of a lot lost.

He nodded, a tiny dip of his head, enough that his eyes didn't leave hers. They pulled her deeper under his spell, held her fast and refused to let her go.

"I…" she stammered, heart thumping, blood racing, and the sensible and cautious part of her began to push through the haze of desire, the heat of her need, and regain ground. "I…"

"You what?" He lowered his eyes to her mouth, as if challenging her to admit that need.

That consuming desire to feel his lips on hers.

"I should call Kyter."

Shit, had she really just said that?

She wanted to scream when he immediately dropped his hand from her face and stepped back, distancing himself.

Stupid sensible part of her.

Said part reminded her that it was possible Talon had a woman already. As if she could forget the way he had called her name. Damn it, but she did keep forgetting though. She kept getting caught up in him, and it was dangerous. She couldn't let herself get swept up in the moment. She needed to maintain some distance between them.

It was for the best.

"I'll tell him your name is Tony."

He scowled again, but there was a twinkle in his eyes. "You really aren't very funny… or original."

"You seem too serious to recognise funny when you see it," she countered, enjoying the sudden lightness between them and the sense of connection it sparked in her.

"Sorry… the past six months haven't done much for my sense of humour." He shoved strong fingers through his unkempt black hair, pushing it back from his face, and all the light left his eyes.

Sucked the funny right out of her with it.

A weight settled on her chest. "You were in Archangel for six months?"

Far longer than she had guessed.

She couldn't imagine what they had done to him in that time, or how he had managed to come through it alive, and seemingly sane. How many times in those long months had he ended up as badly beaten as he had been last night?

Talon nodded and rubbed his hand over his hair again, scrubbing the back of it and making his muscles tense in a teasing way that she struggled to ignore, trying to focus on his story and not his body. It was difficult, but the distant edge his eyes gained, and the way his deep voice dropped to a low whisper was enough to have her focus firmly fixed on his face and his welfare.

"I was there a month or so before the elf prince and that female's brother were guests there."

"That was around six months ago. Which means…" she tailed off, unable to say it, because a shadow flitted across his face, stealing all the colour from his golden skin and making his eyes as cold as a glacier, as distant as the stars.

He bowed his head, and heaved a sigh that had his shoulders trembling. "I was there longer than that."

Talon dug both hands into his hair and grasped his head, his grip so fierce his muscles tensed and veins popped, standing out beneath his skin. His arms shook, and she ached to move closer, to place her hands on his wrists as she had last night and keep him grounded, and with her.

"I…" he rasped and his lips drew back in a grimace that flashed long canines as he growled viciously. "It all sort of blurred… I tried keeping track… guess I failed at that too."

She didn't like the note of resignation and self-damnation in his voice, or the way his strength visibly left him right before her eyes.

Fuck keeping her distance.

Sherry closed the gap between them, brought her hands up and took hold of his forearms without any trace of hesitation, because he needed her.

He needed this comforting touch to chase away all the vicious blows he had been dealt in recent months.

He needed to know that there were still good people in this world, ones who were there for him if he needed them and if he would accept them and their help.

He stilled, his body tense beneath her hands, as solid as a rock, and then slowly lifted his head and looked at her through long inky lashes, his amber eyes questioning her, asking her why she kept reaching for him like this.

She hid nothing from him, wished she was brave enough to tell him in words and not just with her eyes that she did it because she cared, because she wanted to pull him up from that black abyss that kept trying to swallow him and set his feet back on solid ground. She wanted to tell him that until he found his strength again, he could rely on hers.

"Coffee?" She offered him a smile, a small one she hoped would coax him into letting go of his head before he caused any permanent damage.

A hint of a smile curved his lips, and in his eyes she caught the gratitude he couldn't express, the silent thank you aimed at her for not keeping her distance from him, for coming to him and comforting him rather than withdrawing and thinking him crazy and dangerous.

"Feel free to forage for food while I make it." She took hold of his left wrist, brought his arm down and led him into the kitchen.

Heat travelled down her spine, and she swore he was looking at her. She snuck a glance at him and found him staring at her backside. Wasn't he something to someone else? Or maybe he was a bit of a player, and Jayna had just been another lover?

Sherry knew the appeal of the no-strings-attached style of relationship, normally went in for that herself.

So why did the thought of a roll in the hay with Talon followed by a kiss goodbye leave her cold?

She busied herself with the coffee maker while Talon prowled around the small kitchen, taking up far too much space and making it impossible for her to pretend he wasn't there and get her head straight.

And her heart.

She blamed it for her sudden desire to have more than a one night stand with a hot guy.

"Milk, Tony?" She poured two mugs of coffee.

He froze with his head in the refrigerator, withdrew and slowly turned towards her, the scowl back in place.

His deep voice rolled through the room, curled around her and did wicked things to her body.

"Talon," he said with determination, with a hard edge that was both a demand and a command, one that thrilled her as she imagined him ordering her around in the bedroom in that same voice. "Talon. Say it."

A sudden onset of nerves swept through her as she looked into his hard amber eyes, looked at him for all that he was, and realised that if she said his name, the flimsy barrier she had tried to construct between them by avoiding using it would fall.

Leaving her exposed.

He straightened to his full height, towering over her, at least the same height as Kyter's six-five. Talon was broader though, heavy with muscle, cutting an imposing figure as he stared her down, silently demanding she do as he wanted.

"Tiger," she blurted and went to face the coffee mugs again.

Talon moved in a blur of speed, suddenly pressed right against her, and had her cheek in his palm again, bringing her head back around to face his.

"Talon." His tone could have made diamonds it was so hard, so sharp and pressing.

She swallowed hard, trembling from head to toe as she drowned in his amber eyes, watching the gold shimmering among the amber.

Her mouth turned dry.

She swept her tongue across her lips to wet them.

His gaze fell there, grew hungry and heated, and turned the fire up inside her.

"Talon," she whispered.

His eyes shot to hers.

His throat worked on a hard swallow.

"Dear gods," he muttered and just as quickly as he had closed the distance between them, he opened it up again, disappearing into the living room.

She stared at where he had been, reeling from the suddenness of his disappearance, and how shocked he had sounded. How pained.

What the ever living fuck?

He had wanted her to say his name, and then he had reacted as if she had hurt him by saying it, and had fled the room, clearly not wanting to be near her anymore.

Why?

Sherry picked up both coffees and set them back down on the faux granite counter when her hands shook so badly she was in danger of spilling the hot liquid everywhere.

She curled her hands into fists and squeezed them tight, trying to stop them from trembling. If only she could stop her heart from trembling just as easily.

Or stop the pain that echoed in it.

Was it because of this mysterious Jayna? Had she sounded too much like her? Or did he feel he was betraying Jayna by flirting with her?

She stared at the coffee, the pain fading as anger sparked inside her, and the barrier he had torn down by demanding she say his name rose up again around her heart, stronger now.

Screw him.

He wasn't going to play with her emotions like this.

She grabbed the coffees, turned on her heel and swept into the room with her head held high.

And stopped dead when she saw him.

He was attempting to wear a trench in her wooden floor, pacing the length of the room beyond the couch, from the door to her bedroom on her left to the wall on her right.

His right thumb worried his lower lip, his eyes fixed on the floor just a few feet in front of him, and his left arm wrapped across his stomach, his hand clutching his hip with a tight grip.

As if he was trying to hold himself together.

What was bothering him? His time in captivity, or the way he had reacted to her saying his name?

She wanted to know, but there was something else she wanted to know even more.

Something that was bothering her.

She set the coffees down on the low table near him, straightened to face him and said without hesitation, "What else did you fail at?"

He paused mid-step and looked at her, something strange shining in his eyes before he blinked, something she wanted to decipher because it looked to her as if she had caused it and his pacing.

All by simply saying his name.

He frowned at her.

"You said you failed at that too when talking about keeping track of the time… *too*… so what else did you fail at?"

He averted his gaze, his eyes darkening and growing haunted as he stared blankly at the TV screen, and murmured, "I was meant to protect someone."

Her heart hitched. "Someone called Jayna?"

His head whipped around, his amber eyes wide as they met hers.

She looked away from him, doing her best to ignore that hissing in her heart, that pain that radiated through it whenever she thought about this one called Jayna and what she might mean to Talon.

"You shouted her name before you came around last night." She refused to look at him when he moved a step towards her, and backed off, keeping the distance between them steady and the furniture in his path to her, because if he touched her again, her barriers would crumble, and she needed to keep him locked out of her heart.

She needed a little time to get herself back under control and to get it into her head that whatever she felt for him, whatever she wanted from him, it was impossible.

She wasn't going to fall for someone.

Love was painful. Messy. It destroyed people.

It wouldn't destroy her.

He sighed, and she still refused to look at him, because she was weak, and he had far too little clothing on. Damn him. Just hearing him sigh was enough to have a vivid image of his body in her head, an instant replay of how his muscles shifted whenever he drew a deep breath.

"Jayna was... she was a tiger like me... and she was taken with me to Archangel. I was meant to protect her," he whispered, the pain lacing his voice making her want to look at him.

She resisted, needed just a little more time to reinforce the barrier around her heart and make it strong enough to stand against him. He sighed again. Bastard. She swore he knew that it weakened her whenever he did that, put a vision of deliciousness in her head that she wanted to feast on.

"She ended up protecting me." He sagged onto the couch, as if the weight of what had happened was too much for him to bear and he wasn't strong enough to stand while talking about it. "She's the reason I'm here now... free at last."

"She's back at Archangel?" Sherry risked glancing at him, and regretted it when her heart melted at the sight of him staring at the TV, his eyes distant and glassy, filled with pain.

A frown flickered on his brow. "In a way."

The regret in those three words told her not to probe into it, because it would only wound him. He had been hurt enough, and she wouldn't be the one to make him bleed again, not even when she wanted—no, needed—to know what had happened.

And what Jayna had meant to him.

She didn't need to ask to know they had been close, and that the female tiger had meant a lot to him.

Which left her feeling he was way beyond her reach.

But it did nothing to stop her from feeling so drawn to him.

It didn't stop her from feeling they were meant to be.

Her gut was screaming at her though, warning her that only heartbreak lay ahead if she allowed him to get under her skin, or any deeper than he already was.

She had to do something to maintain the distance between them.

She stooped and picked up her phone from the coffee table, and activated the screen.

"Who are you calling?" Talon glared at her phone.

Sherry punched in the number and lifted it to her ear.

"The cavalry."

CHAPTER 8

The cavalry were apparently the jaguar shifter called Kyter and his mate, Iolanthe.

Talon frowned at the blond male as he took agitated strides across the small apartment, his heavy-soled black leather boots loud on the floor.

The second the male had shown up, he had convinced Sherry to give them some time alone and to take a shower so she would feel brighter. Talon had failed to notice that her blue eyes had gained a dullness that wasn't fatigue. It ran deeper than that.

Something was bothering her, and it was hurting her.

The damned jaguar had seen it straight away.

As soon as Sherry had closed the door to the bedroom and the shower had switched on, Kyter had made it perfectly clear that he blamed him for her apparent emotional pain.

He had been silent since.

Iolanthe sat on the arm of the couch, watching her mate with concerned violet eyes as she played with her long blue-black hair, casually braiding it. She had ditched the armour at least, swapping it for a black leather corset and matching tight black leather trousers, coupled with knee-high boots. The hilt of a blade peeked out from behind her right side. She probably had it strapped to the waist of her trousers.

Talon warily kept an eye on her as he stood near the coffee table, because he'd had enough blades stuck in him over the last seven or eight months to last an eternity.

Kyter tossed him another black look, one that accused him all over again.

"I did nothing to her." It felt as if he had said that around a million and one times now.

None of them had changed the way the jaguar looked at him. The male stopped, folded his arms across his dark grey t-shirt, and shifted his booted feet shoulder-width apart, causing his black combat trousers to stretch tight across his thighs.

A fighting position.

As if Talon was stupid enough to attack him. He recalled the male threatening to leave him on the curb for Archangel to find, but he hadn't gone through with it. There was honour in him, and doubt too. He believed that Archangel were up to no good.

It was down to Talon to prove it.

"I don't like you," Kyter muttered.

Iolanthe sighed. "Here we go again."

Her mate glared at her. It was a nice change from him glaring at Talon.

He spoke too soon, because the jaguar's piercing gold gaze came back to land on him.

"I saw the way you looked at her... we both did," Kyter snapped, voice a low growl that had Talon's hackles rising. "You think she's something to you... but I'm not letting it happen."

"Isn't it her choice?" he bit out.

Kyter flashed his fangs. "Don't give me that bullshit. I'm a male... I know what's going on in that head of yours... and what your animal side wants you to do. I'm saying to back the fuck off now because it isn't going to happen."

Talon clenched his fists at his sides and somehow, the gods only knew how, stopped himself from vaulting over the couch and ploughing one of them into the irritating bastard's face.

Trouble was, said irritating bastard was right about one thing.

His tiger did want Sherry, and it wanted her whether she liked it or not. It craved her. Ached for her. And it wouldn't be happy, he wouldn't be happy, until she was his.

He wouldn't rest until then.

But he wasn't doing this the way his nature wanted, he wasn't going to drag her kicking and screaming into his world just because she had been made for him.

"It's her choice," he said again.

Kyter took a hard step forward.

Iolanthe rose to her feet, crossed the room and placed her hand on Kyter's chest, stopping him dead. "Ki'aro... if he hurts Sherry, we will hurt him."

She slid cold violet eyes in Talon's direction and a chill went down his spine.

He held his hands up at his sides. "Look... I have no intention of—"

The door to the bedroom opened.

Everyone looked there.

Sherry stood on the threshold, a beige towel held against her wet golden hair and her blue eyes wide as she looked at each of them in turn.

Those eyes narrowed in suspicion. "Are you talking about me?"

"No," Kyter quickly said, before Talon could utter a word, and at least they were on the same side when it came to keeping some things from her.

For now anyway.

He would find a way to tell her that she was his fated one when she was ready to hear it.

And he was ready to say it.

Sherry gave Kyter a look, huffed and continued on through the living room to the kitchen.

Talon's gaze followed her, raking down her long blonde hair, the wet patch it had left on the back of her white t-shirt, to the snug pale blue jeans that moulded to her pert backside.

Kyter growled.

He refused to take his eyes off her, didn't give a damn if the male hit him for it either. He was sure that Sherry would have a few things to say if Kyter dared to lay a hand on him.

She emerged from the kitchen with a steaming mug of coffee, yawned and padded across the wooden floor to the jaguar.

And boxed him on the arm.

"I chose my apartment for this meeting because it's neutral territory... so no growling at my guest." She swept past Kyter, missing the scowl he aimed at her, and settled on the arm of the couch, twisted on her bottom so she was facing the other way and pressed her bare feet into the seat.

Talon wanted to mention that her apartment wasn't neutral territory, that he had made it his ground while she had been sleeping, and he wasn't particularly proud of it.

There was something a little sad about the spree he had gone on now he was looking back at it, but at the time it had felt like the right thing to do, and his animal instincts had coaxed him into it.

It had been a moment of weakness.

One that had resulted in him rubbing his scent over almost everything in the apartment.

Even her kettle.

She wouldn't be able to smell it, but the jaguar could.

He stared Kyter down, challenging him to say something about it.

The male stared right back, looked as if he was going to tell on him to Sherry, and then huffed and shifted his focus to her.

"You okay?" Kyter said in a soft voice, one filled with concern and affection.

Talon wanted to punch him for it. The bastard was making a point, twisting the knife that sat in his heart because he had failed to notice she had been down about something.

Sherry nodded. "All good now. You were right... a shower was just the medicine I needed."

Talon felt like growling over that one. No. The jaguar didn't get to solve her problems for her, not anymore. He was here now, her fated one, and it was his duty to take care of her and do those things for her. He wanted to solve her problems. He wanted to be the first to notice when she was hurting, or unhappy about something.

He focused on her, using all of his senses to monitor her as he opened himself up for once, allowing his animal side to rise to the fore. It was dangerous, but he had to do it. He needed to be distant from it at a time when he had to stick with tradition and not shift, but he needed to be close to it even more. It would be worth the risk if it paid off and he grew closer to her.

It was that part of him that was most in tune with her, that had recognised her as his mate, and it was that part that would be the key to winning her.

Or losing her.

That didn't bear thinking about.

He needed to keep his head and his cool if he was going to come through this meeting unscathed and with the jaguar still on his side. It was vital. If Kyter turned against him, Iolanthe and Sherry were liable to follow suit.

He wasn't stupid.

He knew he needed all of them, not just Sherry. He needed the strength of Kyter and Iolanthe if he was going to somehow save those he had left behind in Archangel.

His older brother, Byron, had always been destined to lead their pride when their parents passed on to the eternal forest, so Talon had been raised as a warrior, and a strategist, one able to view the world objectively and see fault in the propositions of his alpha and correct them so his pride would only grow stronger and continue.

Talon had learned to apply that ability to all situations.

He didn't have a hope in Hell of surviving if he tried to go back to Archangel alone. So he would rely on others and work as a team with them to form a strong offence. There was strength in numbers. Any tiger knew that. Any shifter knew it.

It was the reason they all ran in packs and prides.

"Bleu should be here soon." Iolanthe's light voice shattered the silence and Kyter checked the watch on his left wrist. The elf glanced at Sherry and smiled. "I gave him your address. I hope you don't mind."

"Not at all." Sherry sipped her coffee and sighed, sounding as if that single taste had been Heaven for her.

Deep inside, he purred that it had. She had experienced happiness from it, a joy that was fresh and new to him. Food was food, drink was drink. They were just basic necessities of life. Yet she felt something strong, powerful and moving, from a single drop of coffee.

His female was an interesting one.

He wanted to know what other foods and beverages stirred such a potent emotional response in her. He wanted to find some of his own, wanted to experience what she had.

There was a knock at the door.

Talon tensed and swung his gaze that way, his bare feet shifting to spread his weight as he sensed a powerful male on the other side of the wooden door and recognised his scent.

One of the elves from Archangel.

A weight suddenly landed on his chest, making his ribcage feel too tight, and he fought for air as he backed away on instinct. He had to leave. Had to run.

He couldn't let them take him again.

Warmth circled his left wrist, gentle and light, soothing the raging need to escape, shift and run, and not stop running.

"Talon?" Her soft voice beckoned him back to the light and he breathed hard, struggling to tamp down the urge to flee.

To survive.

The warmth spread to his cheek, smelled vaguely of coffee, and a hint of vanilla and honey, and gods, he couldn't stop himself from closing his eyes and rubbing that sweet palm, couldn't get enough of the feel of it on his skin and feared it would go away, that she would take away what he needed.

This comforting caress.

He felt eyes on him, watching, studying, judging him, but he didn't care. He nuzzled her palm, rubbed his mouth across it and the fronts of his fangs, unable to get enough, his need only growing with every attempt to satisfy it.

He grabbed her arm and pulled her closer, smoothed his cheek down her arm and buried his face in the crook of her neck.

She gasped.

A strong hand caught his shoulder and yanked him back. "That's enough."

Talon growled and flashed his fangs at the jaguar, and barely leashed the urge to lash out at him and start a fight, one that would determine who would take care of Sherry from now on.

It was only the thought he might frighten her, might drive her away with his violence, that stopped him.

His gaze slid towards her, his heart expecting the worst—that he had already driven her away.

She stood like a statue, one hand tucked against her chest and the other resting on her neck beneath her damp golden hair, covering where he had nuzzled her.

Her wide blue eyes held his.

No trace of fear in them. No disgust.

Just desire.

They were dark with it, her pupils wide black abysses of arousal, and the flush of colour on her cheeks backed them up.

Together with her scent.

Dear gods, he had thought she had torn down all his defences when he had heard her speak his name the first time.

He had been wrong.

The scent of desire mingling with her natural smell, and the need that beat in his blood through hers, had him verging on spilling in his trousers and filled him with a powerful, consuming need to satisfy her, to give her the pleasure she needed and craved.

And bring her the bliss of release.

It was all he wanted, all he knew. It became all of him. His female needed him.

"Sherry, coffee," Kyter said and she almost jumped out of her skin, her eyes leaping to him, and then she hurried away.

Talon growled at Kyter.

How dare he make his mate go away when she clearly needed him?

When he needed her more than anything, more than the beat of his heart and the breath in his lungs?

"Dial it back," the jaguar snapped and shoved him in his bare chest, a gentle tap that shouldn't have moved him but had his back slamming into the wooden doorframe of the bedroom.

Dammit. He was still weak, in no position to fight with Kyter. The male would easily win, and he knew it, was using it to his advantage to assert dominance over him.

"Didn't see her complaining," Talon spat and barely dodged the fist that flew at his face.

The bastard jaguar snarled as he punched straight through the plaster wall where Talon's head had been.

"Oh, for fuck's sake." Sherry stormed into the room, grabbed Kyter by his right shoulder, and hauled him away. She kept pushing him, shoving his chest until he was on the other side of the room to Talon. When she had him backed against the wall, she planted her hands on her hips. "I don't know what your problem with Talon is, but let it go. He's hurting... he lost someone close to him... a woman... and he just wants comfort from me."

Like hell he just wanted comfort from her. What the fuck had given her that impression?

"Jayna was important to him," she whispered.

Damned lightbulb pinged on in his head.

He would have smiled smugly at the jaguar to show him he had figured out why Sherry had been in some sort of emotional distress when he had shown up, but it knocked him on his arse.

She thought Jayna had been something to him.

That he had loved her.

She couldn't have been more wrong.

He wanted to explain everything to her, but not with an audience. When they were alone again, he would set her straight and show her that she was the only female he wanted.

"So what's his story?" An unfamiliar tall elf male dressed in mortal clothing of black jeans and a long sleeved t-shirt jerked his head towards him.

Talon had forgotten about him.

He would have backed off a step if he hadn't been plastered against the wall.

"What's yours?" he bit out, and the stupidly handsome male scowled at him, his violet eyes relaying just how close he was to joining Kyter in wanting to punch him.

If Sherry so much as looked at him, Talon was in danger of losing his shit.

What gods had been at work when they had created elves anyway? Weren't any of them ugly?

"My story is I have a kingdom to help run, and a date with my mate, and I would like to get back to it. I don't see why I had to come here and talk with some rabid cat about his problems." The male shoved his hand through his wild blue-black hair, preening it back from his face in a way that screamed of irritation, the action flashing the fact he wore black elf armour beneath his clothes.

"Bleu." Iolanthe's chastising tone had a wealth of weariness in it that told Talon she was used to this sort of behaviour from her brother. When the male gave her his attention, she hit him with a scowl that made them look frighteningly similar. "Play nice."

The one called Bleu responded to that by crossing his arms over his chest. Tiny black scales rippled across his hands from his wrists and formed a nasty set of black serrated claws over his fingers. They looked sharp. Talon didn't fancy finding out if they were.

"I want to get back to Taryn," Bleu said on a sigh. "It's irritating me."

"You're always irritated." Kyter grinned at the male.

"This from you?" Bleu shot back, his expression deadly serious, but as the two stared at each other, the corners of his lips trembled, as if he wanted to smile too and was having a hard time fighting it.

Kyter shrugged. "I live for it. Life would be boring if I wasn't annoying someone."

"I take it I'm today's customer?" Talon put in and both males shot him down with glares.

"You don't get to play. You're not in this circle." Kyter positively growled the words at Talon, but he had the feeling that the male had added a silent, and reluctant, 'not yet anyway' at the end when he looked at Sherry.

Maybe there was hope for him.

Hope he could foster and encourage to bloom by closing the distance between them all, by opening up and telling them his story.

It was worth a shot anyway.

CHAPTER 9

"I know you're all having trouble believing Archangel has a darker side... but it's true." Talon pushed away from the wall and paced to the oak coffee table.

He scrubbed a hand over his black hair, finding the shortness of it weird and unsettling after it being long for so many months, and tried to figure out how he was meant to make them believe him.

"I'm not." Bleu had all eyes swinging his way. "Sable thinks there is a rotten core to Archangel, and Olivia backed her up. I checked in with them before coming here."

Sable. Olivia?

Talon must have looked as confused as he felt, because the jaguar said, "Sable was an Archangel hunter, but she's slowly making moves to leave so she can be with her mate, the Third King. Olivia worked for them as a doctor, but now she's mated to Prince Loren of the elves."

So the prince had had an ulterior motive when working with Archangel. He had met his mate and had been pursuing her.

"Then Archangel went and captured Loke... although Sable was a little at fault there... but we got him out," Bleu said and that seed of hope that had set root in Talon's heart had a sudden burst of growth.

"Wait... you broke someone out of Archangel?" He stared at the elf male.

Who just shrugged, as if it was nothing. "We broke Loke out, and caused a little havoc. Were you there at the time?"

"I must have been... but I don't remember it. When was this?" He searched his memories, but he couldn't recall a time when there had been any trouble in the facility.

"Around four lunar cycles ago..."

Four months. Talon went back that far. It was all a blur now, but he still felt sure that if something major had happened at Archangel, he would have known about it.

He certainly would have noticed people breaking captives out of the cells.

His eyes slowly widened.

"Unless there were two," he whispered and everyone looked at him as if he had lost his mind, including Sherry. He looked down into her eyes as she perched on the arm of the purple couch again, gathering his thoughts so he could explain himself and get his theory across. "Where I was being held... there was no break in... which means there has to be two cellblocks."

"You were in their headquarters?" Bleu said and Talon nodded, remembered hearing people talking about it as their main facility in London and that a satellite building had been destroyed. The sick bastards had been excited about the captives from that facility being moved to their headquarters. The elf didn't look convinced. "There's only one cellblock there."

Talon shook his head. "Only one that you saw. Where I was being held, it was below the structure, down a service lift. There were labs and a cellblock... white with glass fronts."

"Like the cellblock we broke into." Bleu arched a black eyebrow at him when he growled at the elf. "I am merely saying it as it is. The cellblock is white, with glass barriers. It is down some steps, off a corridor on the basement level."

"No. It's deeper than that. When I was taken there... and when I escaped... I used a service lift in the basement. It went deeper underground, to a facility there."

"A separate facility?" Sherry looked from him to Bleu. "Would Sable know anything about it?"

He shook his head. "I never saw one in the entire time I was in Archangel, and Sable never mentioned one... but I can ask her. If she doesn't know, then the only possible reason would be that Archangel commanders are keeping it secret for some reason."

A secret facility.

Talon didn't like the sound of that.

Was there another side to Archangel, an organisation with a dark agenda hidden within the one who declared themselves dedicated to protecting the innocent fae, immortals and demons?

He had a flash of the facility, and of a thick steel door at the end of a corridor near the cage that had three different security locks and had been guarded by two men at all times. A door that had tugged at his natural curiosity from the moment he had first seen it, because he wanted to know where it led, and why it required such a high level of security. He was sure they were keeping something in there, something they didn't want people knowing about.

"How did you escape?" Kyter pulled him back to the room, studying him closely, golden eyes searching for the answer to the question, a healthy dose of suspicion in them.

Talon closed his eyes as pain welled up from the depths of his heart. "Jayna... they had her in the cage, the room where they would torture and study us... and did something to her... gave her something. When I was thrown in there, she was maddened, and attacked me."

He pressed his hand to his side as his wound ached in response, and fear tried to sink its claws into him again. He shook it off, and focused on talking, and not feeling. They were just words, just information.

"I tried to make her stop... but she wouldn't listen." He opened his eyes and locked them on the jaguar's. "She sacrificed herself so I would have a chance to escape. I... I held her when she took her last breath and... the bastards panicked and rushed into the room to deal with her… and I killed them… I left her there."

Sympathy flared in the male's eyes.

Talon couldn't take it.

A roar burned through him, his animal side unable to handle the pain, stricken with grief all over again, and he unleashed all that agony, let it all pour out of him and didn't care if he scared anyone with it, or how weak it made him look.

He couldn't hold it in.

His knees hit the floor and he arched his chest forwards and roared again, longer this time, until his throat burned. The pain refused to fade, wouldn't release him from its grip, and fur rippled over his skin, the desire to shift and lose himself in his animal side taking hold.

Hands caught his cheeks and held him firm, her knees pressing into his thighs. "Talon."

He sagged, his strength draining out of him, sucked from him by her comforting touch. Her sweet voice coaxed him back from the brink. Gods. He hung his head forwards, unable to bring himself to look at her.

"My brother is going to kill me when I get home," he whispered to her knees.

She smoothed her hands over his shoulders. "Why would he do such a thing?"

He lifted his head and looked into her eyes, searched them so he didn't miss anything. "She was meant to be his bride. I was tasked with meeting her in the fae town and bringing her home to him. Archangel took us both in a raid, and I did my best to uphold my vow to protect her for my brother… but…"

The beautiful look of surprise that flitted across her pretty face, touched with relief, stole his voice.

"Jayna wasn't…" she said and he shook his head.

She hadn't been a lover to him.

They had been close because of everything that Archangel had put them through, and because they had been the only two tigers at the compound, but nothing more than friends.

Even though Archangel had tried their best to make them something more than that.

"If you're both done, and don't need five minutes in the bedroom, can we get on with this?" Bleu growled and Sherry's cheeks burned bright crimson.

Talon had a touch of heat on his too.

It was so easy to forget the rest of the world existed when he was close to her.

"I want to see Taryn," Bleu muttered under his breath.

"You just want to get laid." Kyter grinned wide when the elf turned a growl on him. "Deny it… go on."

Bleu tossed him a black look but didn't deny it.

"Sable will want to know what the tiger does. She'll want in. You know what she's like." Bleu looked from Kyter to Iolanthe, and down to Sherry. They all sighed and nodded in agreement. "Damned little queen does love her action. Of course, you all know that means Thorne will come with her."

"The more the merrier." Talon wasn't going to complain about having Sable's mate in their ranks. He knew of Hell, and he knew of the demon kings that ruled seven realms there. A few mortal hunters would find it hard to take down a demon king in a rage. The male was an asset he was definitely happy to have on their side. "Sable will be able to get us in?"

"Us?" Sherry said, a note of disbelief in her voice. "No… you can't go back there."

"I have to." He lowered his hands to her thighs and then eased them up to her hips, making the most of her sitting on his lap. "I need to go… I need to help the others."

"How many are we looking for?" Kyter moved closer to the back of the couch, but didn't tear Sherry out of his arms, which was progress.

Maybe he could convince the jaguar to loosen the reins and trust him with her after all.

"They took a few with me in the raid on the fae town… a witch, a couple of shifters, one of which I know was a wolf, and the other I think might be a bear but I'm not sure, and there was a demon merc too. They kept him pretty sedated." He looked from Kyter to Sherry. "I have to get them out. I failed Jayna… I can't fail them too."

She looked as if she wanted to say no again.

"You're sure this is wise?" Iolanthe joined her mate. "You take it hard whenever you are only speaking about what happened. What if going back there—"

"I know the risks," he interjected and set his jaw, his teeth grinding together as anger flared, fire sweeping through him in response to her questioning his strength. "It won't happen. I'll keep my head once I'm there. It's the waiting… the needing… I can't take it. I have to make them pay."

"He'll be fine."

Iolanthe looked to her mate as he said that.

Kyter shrugged, lifting the hem of his grey t-shirt. "It's a male thing."

Bleu nodded in agreement.

Iolanthe grumbled, "Stupid male things."

Kyter grinned, flashing short fangs, and patted her shoulder. "You love it really."

She rolled her violet eyes. "Yes, I do so enjoy it when you feel some ridiculous need to hurl yourself into trouble without thinking about the consequences, all because your jaguar nature needs to work off some aggression."

He slung his arm around her, pulled her up to him and kissed her. "I don't hear you complaining when I'm hurling myself into trouble to save this fine arse of yours."

He palmed the backside in question.

Bleu growled, dismay combined with disgust crossing his face. "That's my sister."

"My mate," Kyter shot back with an unrepentant smile. "I trump you, remember?"

"I think we're getting off track again?" Sherry offered, an awkward edge to her expression as she turned back to face Talon. "Sorry… they're always like this."

He shrugged. "No problem."

No problem at all as long as it kept her distracted so she didn't notice the fact she was still sitting on his knees, her hands on his bare shoulders, all nice and close to him.

"Back in a second." Greenish-purple light traced over Bleu's body and he disappeared.

Talon shuddered at the memory of teleporting with Iolanthe, how cold and like death it had felt. Sherry smoothed her hands over his shoulders, regaining his attention, and smiled at him, a small sympathetic one that said she knew what he was thinking.

Bleu reappeared with a firecracker of a dark-haired female slapping at him, landing blows he didn't try to block as he grinned at her, obviously enjoying himself for some reason. Either he was into rough play, or irritating the female was a source of amusement for him.

Her golden-brown eyes flashed fire at the elf. "You bloody know it winds him up when you do that!"

A mighty roar sounded, deafening in volume, and suddenly there was a monster of a male behind the elf. The huge russet-haired brute grabbed the elf's shoulder in one meaty hand, snarled and hurled him backwards through the front door, sending it flying off its hinges.

"Oh, well that's just great!" Sherry shot to her feet, capturing everyone's attention.

Even the demon's.

She jabbed a finger in his direction, fearless despite the sheer size of the male and his appearance. "You're fixing that."

The huge male blinked, red eyes rapidly gaining an edge of regret that Talon wanted to tell him wasn't going to save him.

Sherry stormed towards the demon king, all spit and fire.

And gods, it made Talon hot for her.

She rose up on her toes and slapped the male, leaving a nice red imprint on his left cheek. The demon frowned, his dusky brown horns curling forwards around his ears as he brought his hand up and touched his face.

Aggression.

Talon was damned if he was going to sit there and let the male retaliate.

He was between Sherry and the brute in a flash, blocking the male's path to her.

The demon king eyed him, curling his lip to flash a single fang as he looked him up and down, and then grunted and stomped towards the female who had appeared with Bleu, as if Talon wasn't worth the bother.

Or maybe he had more pressing matters that needed his attention.

She didn't fight when the demon dragged her into his thickly muscled arms like she was a ragdoll and smothered her with his bare chest, clumsily petting her long black hair.

"Mine," the demon muttered.

The little female sighed, the most exasperated one Talon had ever heard.

Bleu picked himself up off the floor in the hallway outside the apartment, shook off the blow, and staggered back into the room holding his head. He was bleeding, a long gash down his left temple and cheek dripping crimson. In Talon's opinion, the elf was lucky the demon hadn't ripped him to shreds.

It wasn't wise to take things from demons.

Especially their mates.

Bleu muttered something in a foreign lyrical tongue and pinned hard violet eyes on the demon's back.

"You started it." A muffled feminine voice came from somewhere in the tangle of the demon's arms. She grunted and the male jerked backwards several times as she tried to free herself, but he refused to release her. "Oh, let me go, you big oaf! I'm not bloody going anywhere and you've made your point."

He still didn't let her go.

"Mine."

"Great, now you've broken him…" she muttered and Talon thought he heard her sigh again. "Thank you *so* much, Bleu."

Just the sound of his female saying the elf's name was enough to have the demon growling, the dusky brown horns that sprouted from just above his pointed ears curling further, following the curve of his ears downwards, and their tips growing sharper as they twisted around like a ram's. Huge dark leathery dragon-like wings burst from his bare back, knocking a few ornaments on the sideboard against the wall over. He looked over his wide shoulder at the elf, bared fangs on a snarl, and tucked her even closer to his chest.

"Squashing me now." Her voice was strangled.

The demon instantly loosened his hold, caught her shoulders and pushed her back to arm's length. His glowing red eyes ran over her, checking every inch of her, worry flashing in them.

She sighed and smoothed her palms along his jaw. "Not hurt. Not going anywhere. Stop being all growly."

The demon snorted and muttered something in the demon tongue. She sighed again.

"I love *you*, dumbass." She followed that up with a light slap to his cheek. "Hold on to that rage though… because I just came up with the most amazing plan ever."

Who was this female?

She turned a high beam smile on the entire group.

"I know how to get the kitty's friends back."

Kitty? He had the sinking feeling she was referring to him. It was bad enough when people called him cat, or when Sherry had been calling him Tony. Kitty was a whole new level of condescension and one he wasn't going to put up with.

"*Talon*. I'm not a cat… not a damned cartoon on a cereal box… and I'm *definitely* not a kitty. I'm a tiger… and unless you want to get up close and personal with my tiger form, I suggest you call me Talon."

"Down, Tiger." She winked at him. "See what I did there?"

He sighed.

"Sable." She held her hand out, jerked it in the air as if shaking his, and planted it against her black-leather-clad hip. "Nice to meet you."

Sable and Iolanthe obviously shopped at the same store. Both of them wore black leather trousers, but Sable had chosen a simple black t-shirt for her top half. An entire arsenal of weapons that included a long silver knife and a compact folding crossbow hung around her slender waist.

The demon brute had foregone a shirt entirely. He towered behind Sable, his chest a wall of bare muscle and his tight burgundy leathers looking fit to burst as they stretched over his tree trunk legs.

"Thorne," he grunted, and curled one hand over Sable's left shoulder, pressing dark claws into her pale skin. "Mine."

"I got the memo." Talon had the feeling that Thorne acted this way around any new male, and constantly around Bleu for some reason.

Thorne jerked his chin towards Sherry. "Yours."

Sherry blushed a thousand shades of red.

"Well… no… um… no." She didn't sound so sure, which was a victory for Talon.

She wanted him, just as he wanted her.

Sable petted Thorne's hand. "So here's the plan—"

"I'm going into Archangel." Talon cut her off and didn't back down when she glared at him.

"Not a wise idea."

"It is," Sherry said and he couldn't stop his eyes from leaping to her, or the shock that rippled through him. She smiled softly. "I don't want you going back there, but you know the building, and you know where your friends are being held. If you're right, and there's a secret part of the building, Sable will need you there to show her the way."

Sable cursed, a string of them that had her mate's eyebrows rising.

She went through every obscenity imaginable, and then reluctantly sighed. "If that's true, then the tiger comes with us… but it means a change to my plan."

"What sort of change?" Bleu moved into the room, edging to his right, keeping his distance from the demon.

"I'm on the way out with Archangel. If we're going to get the tiger in, we'll need help. Emelia has good standing with the organisation, and she's taking over my team, which makes her the perfect candidate to be the one who captures the tiger."

"Wait… what?" Talon's blood ran cold. "*Capture* me?"

Sable nodded. "How else do you plan to get back into Archangel without them locking it down? If you go barging in there, you'll never get your friends out. Bleu can't teleport you in, douse the lights, and get you and your friends back out. It would be too much of a drain on his powers and would set off alarms all over the building. Hell, even with Iolanthe helping, it would be too risky. We need to focus on the getting you all out part… which means you need to sneak in."

By being caught. He didn't like the sound of that.

He had no reason to trust Sable, or this Emelia character.

"Look… I get it… I'm with Archangel, and they're enemy number one, but I'm mated to a demon, and I'm allied with a lot of different species now… and if Archangel are up to something, I want to know about it, and I want my friends at Archangel to be aware of it too. Emelia needs to see what's going on." Sable stepped out from her mate's shadow, her golden eyes meeting Talon's, sincere and determined. "Word on the grapevine is Archangel are still looking for you. It's the perfect opportunity to get you back inside. Emelia catches you, and takes you in. You'll lead her to your friends, and I'll create a diversion with Thorne to keep everyone busy. When you're in position, you'll contact Bleu and Iolanthe—"

"And me," Kyter interjected.

"And Kyter." She didn't miss a beat. "They'll help you get your friends out."

"I'm going too," Sherry said, and Talon opened his mouth to tell her she damned well wasn't, but her jaw tensed and her blue eyes narrowed on him. "I'm going."

Sable's eyes lit up. "I have the perfect job for you!"

He wanted to tell Sherry no, that he didn't like the idea of her going into Archangel because it was dangerous and he needed to protect her. He held his tongue though, because he could read in her eyes and feel in the trickle of emotions that ran from her and into him, how much she needed to be there with him. He silently promised that he would be there if she needed him, he would keep her safe.

He wouldn't fail her.

"You can borrow some of my Archangel gear," Sable said and Sherry nodded. "We'll get you in through the roof access and you can meet up with Emelia after she's left Talon with the others."

"What do you want me to do?" There was a wobble in Sherry's voice that betrayed her nerves, and the need to tell her no kicked back to life inside him, stronger this time, so fierce it was a struggle to tamp it back down.

"I want you to get important information for me." Sable's expression shifted, growing warmer, yet determined, and Sherry's courage rose in response, her nerves fading. The ex-Archangel huntress had clearly been a leader, and he admired her ability to inspire people and give them strength. "You'll meet up with Emelia after she drops Talon off in the cells and she'll take you to the central files division. You should be able to use one of the terminals there to find out why Talon and the others were taken. I'll give you a USB drive so you can download anything you find that might be useful."

Sherry nodded.

Talon didn't like the sound of that.

"Just download whatever you find and get out of there. We can look at it when we've met up and we're safe." His desire to have her get in and out as quickly as possible was partly because he wanted her safe.

And partly because he wasn't sure whether Archangel had discovered his secret.

He didn't want Emelia, or any of the others learning about it.

And he didn't want Sherry finding out about it before he had a chance to tell her himself.

"I'll meet up with you," he said.

Sherry shook her head, a flicker of fear entering her blue eyes again. "No. I want you out of there as soon as possible."

That touched him, even as it riled him. She wasn't questioning his ability as a warrior, and she wasn't saying she didn't need him to protect her, but it felt that way.

"I'm finding you and bringing you out of there with me. I'm not going to let Archangel do anything to you, Sherry. I'm not going to leave you unprotected." He stepped closer to her, so she had to tip her head back to keep her eyes on his, and refused to back down even when the softer side of himself, the part that was in tune with her, warned he was upsetting her.

And exposing himself to the others.

Their eyes pierced him, their unspoken questions ringing in his ears. What was Sherry to him?

He didn't want them knowing the answer to that question, even when part of him knew they already did, and that his little outburst had only confirmed it all for them.

"Talon," Sherry whispered and placed her hand on his chest, right over the tiger inked on his left pectoral.

That touch unravelled him.

All of his anger washed out of him as if she had lifted a barrier, his need to fight her in order to keep her safe running from him with it, and he could only stare down into her blue eyes, catching the resolve that flashed in them, among the other emotions.

Ones that stole his breath.

Ones that told him things she couldn't say.

She liked his desire to protect her.

She understood it.

Because she felt the same way.

Kindred spirits.

They both wanted to know the other one was safe, wanted to protect and shield them, and stop anything from happening to them.

Gods, there had never been a female who had wanted to fight in his corner, who wanted to protect him.

Females had always looked at him as a protector, a warrior, one who would keep them safe.

Now a female was looking at him as an equal, as something important enough to her that she wanted to be the protector, the warrior, the one who would keep him safe.

It warmed his heart.

Had he really only known this fierce, beautiful female for a few short hours?

It felt as if he had known her his entire life, that he had always been aware of her.

Waiting for her.

Needing her above anything else.

She was the other half of his soul, everything he had been missing, and now she was within his reach.

He only had to overcome one hurdle and she would be his forever.

One that felt impossible to leap.

One that might take her away from him forever.

CHAPTER 10

Talon was acting strange.

After they had fixed her front door, and the others had left, he had kept his distance from her. He looked troubled as he stared at the TV, and he hadn't heard a word she had said when she had asked if he was hungry.

Now she stood at the end of the couch, watching him as his coffee went cold on the wooden table, waiting for him to notice her.

Something was troubling him.

"Talon?" She inched closer.

His amber eyes snapped up to her, focused and he blinked. "Sorry. You say something?"

Was he just anxious to get going on the plan? Nervous that he was going to play bait for Archangel?

It scared the hell out of her.

Sherry sat on the arm of the couch, planted her feet on the cushion, and rested her chin on her upturned palm. "Are you worried?"

He shook his head, but that troubled edge to his eyes remained. "Archangel can't hold me again. I won't let it happen."

"I won't either," she said, and his eyes widened a little, a ripple of warmth and light chasing through them before the darkness closed back in. "During the meeting… you mentioned you had a brother."

He nodded, sighed and leaned back into the couch, tipping his chin up and his face towards the ceiling. Obviously he had a brother that exasperated him, was trouble enough that just thinking about him had Talon's mood degenerating. Or was it because he had failed to keep Jayna safe?

"Is he going to be pissed at you?" She studied his face, trying to discern from it how he felt about his brother.

His eyes told her everything as they slid towards her, overflowing with weariness and the smallest hint of fear.

"Probably," he muttered, and then added, "Definitely."

Another long sigh escaped him, shifting his bare chest, tempting her eyes to fall there.

Talon closed his eyes.

"My older brother Byron is my pride's alpha. I'm his second in command, not a very enviable job when it involves dealing with him. He can be… moody. Normally, a small group of females are sent together with a couple of our males, warriors, to visit another pride and return with a bride. This time, Byron tasked me with meeting Jayna and bringing her to the village." He grimaced, and Sherry had the feeling he was imagining how upset his brother was going to be when he returned home and told him that Jayna was gone. Her heart whispered that his reluctance to go home was about more than his brother's anger though.

It was because he had failed, and he didn't want his brother to know about it, or the pride.

She could understand why. He was second in command of an entire tiger pride, an important position by the sounds of it. When he returned and revealed what had happened, his ability to hold that position would come into question, along with his abilities as a warrior.

How could he be expected to protect his pride if he couldn't protect a single female?

"Good job I can't go back yet, huh? Not with Archangel still looking for me. Guess they're a blessing in disguise in a way, stopping me from having to go back and face my brother's wrath. I should probably thank them when they capture me again." He cracked his eyes opened and looked at her, but there wasn't an ounce of humour and not a trace of light in them.

He looked tired, worn down just thinking about things.

Was it only the thought of heading into Archangel and returning home that was hurting him?

Or was it something else?

Whatever it was, she wanted to free him of its chains.

She wanted to take away his pain.

"Talon—"

"Do me a favour," he cut her off and she nodded. His handsome face shifted, dark slashes of his eyebrows falling as he turned his head towards her, suddenly so serious that a shiver went down her spine. "Don't look at my file… and don't let anyone else see it. Keep it separate… or don't download it at all. I don't want the jaguar or the others seeing it."

She had a feeling that he didn't want her seeing it either.

"Why?" she whispered, certain that he wouldn't answer her, but needing to ask.

He stared at her in silence.

Eventually sighed.

Looked away, fixing his gaze back on the ceiling.

"I have a secret, and I need to keep it."

That just made her want to press him even more. What sort of secret? Why did he want to keep it from her too?

The shimmer of nerves that entered his eyes, and seemed to echo inside her, connected the dots in her head and his behaviour since the meeting had ended suddenly made sense.

Because his demeanour hadn't changed since everyone had left.

It had changed the moment Sable had announced Sherry's part of their grand plan.

He had been worried since then, slowly withdrawing into himself because he felt a need to protect himself, and that was manifesting in him pulling away from her.

That gave her the strength to let it go, to place her trust in him and not let this secret bother her or stand between them. Everyone was entitled to their secrets. She had plenty herself and she knew Kyter had a few that only Iolanthe knew.

Perhaps one day, Talon would be ready to tell her his secret.

She stared at him, reeling from that thought, and the need that went through her in response, the deep desire to be that close to him.

To stay with him.

Shit, she needed to keep things lighter than that between them, couldn't let them get heavy. Hadn't she vowed that she wouldn't fall in love?

His eyes slid back to her.

A sudden need to say something rushed through her, as if he would know her ridiculous thoughts if she sat there in silence, and she didn't want him to know how deeply he affected her.

"Do you have other family?" She fiddled with a fraying patch on the hem of her pale blue jeans, teasing the threads. "You mentioned Byron was your older brother... do you have a younger one?"

He shrugged. "In a way. I have a younger sister too."

"What's it like having brothers and sisters?" Damn, had she sounded envious?

The tension that had been building inside him seemed to flow out of him and he relaxed into the couch, turning his head towards her, a light back in his amber eyes. "You don't have any?"

Sherry shook her head, a flare of regret bursting inside her, together with a question that had always plagued her. If she'd had brothers and sisters, would things have been different?

"They can be a pain... but I like having family... I think it's an instinct thing. Might be a pride thing. Feline shifters like to have others around." He almost smiled.

She did smile at that. "Kyter certainly does. He tries to pretend he's cool with it all, but in reality, he gets weird if we're not around... like antsy."

Talon dipped his head to his left, his eyes wide and eyebrows high on his forehead as he clearly considered it. "It's a pride thing. The jaguar views you as his pride, and he gets restless when you're unaccounted for... and how the fuck did you end up working for a shifter in a club that is for immortals anyway?"

He looked as if he had been dying to ask that question for a long time now and was relieved it was finally out in the open. Curiosity killing her cat? She scrubbed that thought. He wasn't her cat.

Sherry looked deep into his eyes, catching how badly he wanted to know the answer to that question. She didn't want to answer it.

She didn't want to think about how she had ended up at Underworld.

Talon shifted closer, concern washing across the rugged lines of his face. "You're upset."

She shook her head, but stopped herself halfway through and sighed instead. "It's not a pretty story, Talon."

He leaned closer still and placed his hand on her knee, his eyes sincere as he held her gaze and softly murmured, "But it's one I would like to know."

Was it so important to him? The way he was looking at her answered that, telling her that he was being honest, truly wanted to know how she had come to be at Underworld. He wanted to know about her.

"You don't have to tell me if—"

"I ran away from home," she cut him off and he frowned at her. She held her hand up when he opened his mouth to speak, because if she was going to do this, if she was going to bare this part of herself, she needed to do it quickly, like ripping off a sticking plaster. "When I was nine, my mum died in a car accident. I was in the car with her. My dad... he took it hard. It was like all the light went out of him with her... and he was never the same again. It killed him. He fell apart... and I realised how much he had loved her."

His amber eyes filled with sympathy.

"It was hell after that." She lowered her eyes to her knees, placed both hands over them and stared at them. "Dad blamed me for her death... hated me... he pretended to be fine around my teachers and others, but when we were alone... he couldn't even bring himself to look at me. I lost count of the number of times he told me he wished I had died instead."

"Fucker," Talon snarled.

She closed her eyes. His fingers flexed against her knee.

Before he could utter a word about her stopping, she said, "I'm doing this... just... I need to finish."

He didn't say a word, but she could feel how much he wanted to speak, how angry he was about how her father had treated her. Her father had been a broken man. Love had utterly destroyed him. In the end, it had almost destroyed her too.

"It wasn't any way to treat you," he growled, and she let him have that one.

"He was hurting... had lost someone he loved. I was hurting too. I would lash out at him in return, and then we would fight... and it would be ugly... and all because we had both lost someone we loved."

She sighed and couldn't bring herself to look at him as he stared at her, his eyes boring into her, as if he could see how it had coloured her opinion of love and he didn't like it. Sometimes, she didn't like it either. Sometimes, she wanted to take the risk and fall for someone.

Like now.

"I ran away from home at fifteen. I stole his motorbike after we'd had this big fight and he had said he wanted me gone. I was so upset... I lost control of the bike and crashed it into a ditch." Sherry lifted the right leg of her jeans, revealing the start of the scar that ran up her shin to her knee, and Talon stared at it, all the fires of Hell raging in his eyes, his jaw set hard and eyebrows drawn low. She carefully smoothed her jeans back down, and he lifted his eyes back to hers. She didn't look away from him this time, because she needed to know he was there with her, needed the comfort of his presence and his strength. "My dad found me in the hospital and rather than being concerned about me and my fucked up leg, he was pissed about the fact I had trashed his bike."

Talon lowered his hand to her right shin, stroked it up and down in a way that both soothed and seared her, making her itch to feel his hand on her bare skin. His eyes held hers, darker now, conveying the way he felt about her father.

Pretty much the same way she felt about him.

She hated him.

"I ran away again at nineteen, and ended up in London. Spent a year or so on the streets, roughing it… until I was caught stealing food from the bins behind Underworld." She smiled at that, still able to remember being dragged through the empty club and brought up in front of a very groggy and pissed off Kyter. He had been more angry about being woken than the fact she had been going through the trash. "Rather than turning me over to the authorities, he gave me a place to stay in exchange for me working for him… he pretty much saved my arse."

At the time, she hadn't understood why. It had only been after she had learned he was a jaguar shifter, and all his staff were immortals too, that she had realised he had done it because he had a habit of taking in strays, was creating his own small pride from non-humans who no longer had a place to call home.

People like him.

"How long have you known your boss is a shifter?" He sounded curious again, and she risked a glance at him, caught the glimmer of it in his eyes as he watched his hand skimming up and down her leg.

Did he like touching her?

"Um… like… maybe eight years or so. I don't really remember."

"And you stayed?" He lifted his eyes to hers.

Sherry smiled. "Of course… why wouldn't I?"

He frowned at her. "Just… it must have been a shock."

"It was, but I always had the feeling something was off. I mean, the gym at Underworld has plastic barrels in it and knotted ropes, and there was a huge stuffed bear at one point that looked a little worse for wear." Her smile widened when she thought about the one time she had caught Kyter in his jaguar form with that bear in a death grip, his hind paws kicking at its stomach. When he had finished, she had teased him by petting him and congratulating him on being a big bad kitty and killing the bear. It hadn't gone down well. "Underworld... it's my home now... and everyone there is my family."

He pulled a face. "If you ask me, your big brother is an overprotective pain in the arse."

She giggled. "He can be a little like that... but he's saved my arse plenty of times now... I have to give him something back and if it's putting up with a jaguar who wants to kill anyone who might hurt me, I'll live with that."

Talon averted his gaze and blew out a long sigh, and might have muttered something under his breath, something about not being out to hurt her.

"Must be nice having real family though," she said in a low voice, trying to imagine what his life was like.

Kyter had painted a grim picture of his pride, but Cavanaugh had made his sound wonderful, like a close-knit community. One big family.

"In some ways... not in others." Talon tipped his head back and grimaced. "Byron is not going to be happy with me."

Something about the way he said that annoyed her and made her hate his brother even though she had never met him. Byron should be glad to have Talon back, alive and safe, and not blame him for what Archangel had done to Jayna. She had the horrible feeling that Byron was like her father though, and liable to hurt Talon just as her father had hurt her, making his life Hell because of what had happened to his bride.

Talon's amber gaze slid downwards to land on her, and he rolled his head towards her. "What's wrong?"

He always seemed to know when she was upset. How? Could he sense it in her?

She didn't want to talk more about her family, and didn't want to hurt him by talking about his brother either, reminding him what lay ahead for him.

She settled for a safer topic.

One that was playing on her mind.

"I'm a little nervous." Her pulse quickened when his right eyebrow rose and she suddenly realised that he could interpret that in a thousand ways— including that she was nervous about being alone with him. "About going into Archangel."

The wicked hunger that had been building in his eyes dissipated, concern replacing it.

"I know," he murmured and ran his eyes over her, over every part of her except her face. He was avoiding eye contact. Why? She frowned at his face, at the struggle written in every strong line of it. He sighed, closed his eyes, and then opened them and met hers. "I can feel it in you... I can feel when you're worried... or upset... or happy... and I can feel when you're nervous."

Sherry had the feeling that was meant to surprise her, or terrify her. Kyter picked up on her emotional signals too, and even Cavanaugh could at times. The bastards could read her like a book if she wasn't guarded with her emotions.

She stared at Talon, her gut telling her that his ability to sense things in her ran deeper than Kyter and Cavanaugh's talent for pissing her off by prying into her private feelings.

Dangerously deeper.

The big demon had said that she was Talon's, and Talon hadn't denied it.

He had been swift to protect her, had risen to all the bait that Kyter had tried to hook him with too, and had forgotten their company from time to time, seemingly lost in her and unaware of the world.

Shit, hadn't she felt the same?

It was dangerously easy to lose herself in Talon and forget the world.

She didn't want to think about the how of it, or the why, but she could sense things about him too.

Like the fact he was nervous again.

"You'll blend in." His deep voice sank into her, warmed her right down to her bones and teased her senses, chasing away the doubts and her fears, and crushing her ability to keep some distance between them. She met his gaze, fell into it and into the dream of just sliding off the arm of the couch and into his arms, and forgetting everything for a while. She wanted to be closer to him. His hands twitched against his thighs, as if he wanted to pull her into his arms, wanted that same moment of madness as she did. "You're human and they won't suspect you if you're with that huntress."

She ignored the sharp way he had mentioned her species. If he had been trying to remind himself that she was just a little mortal and not a beautiful tigress, he had failed, because the hunger that had fled his eyes was building again like a storm.

A storm she knew would light them both up and change their lives forever if they let it crash over them.

Sherry curled her hands into fists on her knees, ignored the voice at the back of her head that chanted at her about keeping her distance, about how this would only end in heartbreak, and that love was painful, and dragged her courage up.

Because she was about to do something crazy, leaping into the lion's den to get information for the man in front of her. She was going to risk her life for him, because deep inside she knew he was worth it.

And she was going to risk her heart too.

For one night with him.

She couldn't dance around it any longer, and it felt stupid to deny herself something she wanted. This wasn't about love. This was about desire. Attraction. Need. She had never been afraid to scratch itches whenever they had walked into her life before, and she wasn't going to be afraid now. She was still here. Still standing. This wasn't going to turn into anything. It was just satisfying the hunger she felt, one she knew he shared.

Just one night.

She swore it would be enough.

She swore she wouldn't fall for him.

It was just about lust.

Scratching that itch.

Her mouth didn't get the memo.

"I'm not nervous that people will know I'm not with Archangel... I'm worried something will happen to you."

He just stared at her.

Shit. What the fuck had made her say that? Lust. Not love. *Lust!* Damn it all to Hell. She wasn't meant to be feeling anything soft for him, thought she had mastered those emotions and managed to get it into her head and her heart that this was just physical release, just a roll in the hay. Fuck.

Fear was swift to rise and swamp her, that voice screaming at her in a mocking tone, telling her she had been a fool, had just laid it all out there, baring the softest part of her, the side she had meant to keep locked away and hidden. Protected.

Idiot.

She shot to her feet and paced away from him. "Pretend you didn't hear that."

He was on his feet in a flash, and across the room in the next second, hemming her in against the cream wall.

He pressed his palms against it on either side of her shoulders and leaned in close.

"I cannot." He lifted one hand and caught her cheek, smoothed his palm across it and sent shivers dancing over her skin, a tremble that carried heat in its wake that soothed her fear and tamed that voice. She lifted her eyes to his. They were bright gold, mesmerising. Beautiful. She couldn't catch her breath as she stared up into them and his words curled around her. "You want me."

She wanted to deny that.

"Don't," he whispered and traced his thumb across her cheek, his bright amber gaze following it, filled with fascination. "I can feel you... I can feel your need... and it's as fierce as my own."

It was?

Did he feel as if he was on fire, would burn to ashes if he didn't do something?

His eyes met hers again, stole her breath as they told her everything, that this was about more than lust. More than desire.

This crazy thing between them ran as deep as their blood.

As their souls.

She wanted to tell him how she felt, but he stole the words right out of her mouth when he leaned in close, slid his hand around the nape of her neck and clutched it, and brought his lips near to hers, husking in the most earnest and heartfelt voice.

"Gods, I've never needed anyone the way I need you."

CHAPTER 11

She shouldn't do this.

She really shouldn't.

But the thought of what Talon was about to do by allowing Archangel to capture him again, the thought that she might never see him again, seized hold of her and made her act.

Screw the consequences.

He was right, and she wanted him. She felt the same way as he did.

She had never needed anyone the way she needed him.

Sherry tilted her head up, captured his lips and swallowed his gasp in a kiss.

A kiss that stayed soft for as long as it took for him to catch up and realise what was happening.

The second he did, his grip on the back of her neck tightened and he hauled her against him, his mouth dominating hers in a wicked yet wonderful way. She melted into his kiss, placed her hands on his powerful shoulders and drew him closer still, because she couldn't get close enough to him.

His bare chest pressed against hers, and she couldn't contain the moan that rolled up her throat when he groaned and deepened the kiss, as if just feeling her against him had given him a hit of pure pleasure.

His tongue stroked the seam of her lips and she opened for him, wasn't sure she could keep any part of her closed off any longer as he went to war on her defences, stripping them all down with the ferocity of his kiss and the need it conveyed, and the way his body pressed against hers and his hand held her nape.

As if he didn't want to let her go.

Couldn't bear it if she slipped out of his grasp.

That feeling grew in her too, a fear that he might let her go when she needed him so badly she couldn't breathe, couldn't keep still in his arms. She wriggled against him, rubbing her chest against his, and looped her arms around his neck.

He slid one hand down to her backside and she moaned and trembled as he palmed it, large hands kneading her flesh, making her aware of his strength.

Aware of the fact she had never slept with a non-human.

Would it feel different?

Talon broke away from her lips and pressed his forehead against hers, his breath sawing from his lips.

"You're afraid," he whispered, hoarse and husky, sending another ripple of pleasure rolling down her spine.

She went to shake her head, and stopped herself. "I… I've never done this with a…"

It seemed so stupid saying that out loud.

This wasn't her first rodeo, and she was fairly certain shifters didn't really differ that much from a human, other than his strength. He wasn't going to go all tiger on her. She knew that much from overhearing conversations between Kyter and Cavanaugh about their saucy interludes with their mates.

Talon drew back and dazzled her with a grin, one that lit up his eyes and made her realise this was the first time she had seen him smile.

And she had been the one to make him do it.

With her stupid worries.

"I'll be gentle," he murmured and before she could slap his chest and chastise him for not taking this seriously, he bent and scooped her up into his arms.

It would have been the most romantic thing to ever happen to her.

Except Talon grunted and hissed through his teeth.

She didn't weigh that much, did she?

"What's wrong?"

He shook his head. "It's nothing."

Like hell it was nothing. "You sounded hurt."

Her eyes widened as it hit her.

"Put me down." She pushed at his bare chest but he tightened his grip on her, pinning her against his hard body and restraining her legs. "You're going to open that wound again if you're not careful, and then…"

She blushed. Hard. It didn't help when his lips curled in a sly smile, one that said he knew what she had been about to say.

He leaned in and nuzzled her cheek, peppered it with kisses that reignited the fire in her and made her forget what they had been talking about or why she had been worried.

"One little wound isn't going to stop this from happening, Sherry." His lips teased her cheek and her neck as he spoke each word, stirred that fire in her blood until she was burning for him. "I'm having you."

The way Talon said that made it sound so possessive, made her feel he was talking about more than just having her now, for this one moment.

It rang warning bells in her head but his lips worked magic on her throat and silenced them, filled her head with the hum of pleasure instead as she leaned into his mouth and savoured the shivers that tripped over her skin with each kiss.

He turned and carried her towards the bedroom, and her eyes slipped shut, her will to resist melting out of her and leaving her boneless in his arms, craving more from him. Damn, he was good. Better than good. Just his lips on her throat was enough to have her soaring towards release. She couldn't wait to find out what that mouth would feel like on other parts of her body.

When they reached the bed, he set her down on it and continued his assault on her throat. He kissed it harder, laved it with his tongue and sent her flying higher. His lips traced her collarbone and then he swept them up to her ear and sucked on the lobe. She moaned and shuddered, throbbing low in her belly as the fire in her grew hotter.

It burst into a wildfire when his tongue stroked the back of her neck, near her hairline, and she cried out, unable to contain herself.

Talon froze.

Breathed hard against her nape.

His arms shook violently, making the mattress tremble as he supported himself on them.

Something was wrong.

"Talon?" she whispered and he pushed away from her.

"Just need a second." He rose onto his feet and paced across the room, disappearing into the living room.

She stared at the doorway, her eyebrows pinned high on her forehead. What?

She touched the back of her neck, shivered as she remembered how good his tongue had felt there. How right.

And how, for a heartbeat, she had wanted him to bite it.

Had he picked up on that desire?

Or had she picked up on his need to bite her there and interpreted as her own?

She decided to put the back of her neck off limits, at least until she understood what was going on.

She wasn't going to let one little hiccup ruin this moment though.

She stripped off her top, stood and removed her jeans. Her socks followed, and then her underwear. She stared at the bedroom door, heart drumming against her chest, nerves rising again. She quashed them, set her jaw and set her sights on the guy prowling around in her living room.

Talon wasn't getting away that easily.

She wanted him, and she was damned well going to have him.

Sherry sauntered towards the door.

He turned the second she entered the living room.

His amber eyes widened, but the shock in them lasted all of a second before desire took over, dilating his pupils until they devoured almost all of his irises. Hunting her. She trembled in response as instinct told her she was in danger, that this powerful man wanted her and nothing on this planet was going to stop him this time.

He growled, flashing short fangs, and prowled towards her, muscles shifting in a seductive symphony with each stride.

When he was close, he launched at her and caught her around the waist. She gasped as her back hit the mattress and his weight pressed down on her, pinning her there. A little thrill ran through her at the thought he was caging her, making it clear he wasn't going to let her escape.

She struggled beneath him, pressing her hands to his chest and trying to push him off her, a wicked sort of need in command, a deep desire to push him a little and reap the rewards.

On another snarl, he caught her wrists and pinned her arms above her head.

Her chest rose as her back arched in response to her new position, and he groaned and dropped his eyes to her breasts. Hunger flared in them, a dark need that she ached for him to satisfy.

He dropped his head and she cried out in pleasure as he tugged her right nipple into his mouth, teasing it hard with his teeth before wrapping his lips around it and sucking on it. He groaned and shuddered, and she trembled as he pressed his hips down against hers, and she felt his thick length.

Fuck, she needed that inside her.

She needed to feel his strength, needed him to take control and show her just how powerful he was.

How primal and wicked.

He groaned as if he had felt her need, her desires, and released her wrists. He skimmed his hands down her arms and feathered kisses down her stomach, worshipping her body. She tangled her hands together above her head and gave him total control, drank in the way his lips traced her flesh and the dizzying emotions they stirred in her, need and a hunger she had never experienced before that combined with a sensation that only this man could ever satisfy them.

No other would ever be enough for her.

She wriggled as he stroked the fingers of his left hand down her side, and then stilled as they danced across her belly.

The first press of them between her thighs had her hips shooting off the bed.

Talon chuckled and kissed her hip.

He rose off her, straddling her left leg, pinning it to the bed, and the feel of his eyes on her had her opening hers, responding to the demand to look at him. She stared into bright golden eyes, bit her lip and trembled as he stared back at her, a silent promise in his gaze.

A vow that he was going to love her so thoroughly she wasn't going to be able to think straight for days, let alone walk anywhere.

His fingers teased her again, stroked her plump lips and sent another bone-melting blast of pleasure through her.

She kept her eyes on his, and her hands above her head, placed herself completely at his mercy.

His eyes remained locked with hers as he ran two fingers over her sensitive nub and it tensed, eager for more. His eyes grew darker, hooded as he watched her and touched her, and hell, she wasn't going to last long with him looking at her like that.

He brushed his fingers back and forth over her pert bead, sending wave after wave of bliss shooting through her, and she slowly raised her hips into his touch, couldn't stop herself from seeking more, from trying to goad him into giving her what she needed. Those firm lips curled at the corners and he picked up the pace, caressing her faster, harder, sending her spinning out of her mind as she gripped the bedclothes and moaned, shook all over and lost herself.

Need mounted, seizing control.

"Talon," she moaned, trembling beneath him, belly tensing and thighs quivering, aching for release.

He stroked her harder, flicking his fingers over her, an onslaught she couldn't withstand for much longer.

His eyes held hers, that dark promise still filling them, but there was something else in them now, something fiercely possessive.

He slowed his assault and she was about to reprimand him when he stole her voice by tugging on the ties of his trousers with his other hand and freeing his cock. She moaned as he ran his hand down the thick length, revealing the dark blunt head. It shimmered with his need in the low light, and she trembled as he rubbed his thumb over the head, smearing the moisture into it as he stroked her, teased her with his touch and the delicious vision of him caressing himself.

Too much.

She tipped her head back, ready for release to take her.

Talon stole his touch away.

Her eyes snapped open, vicious words ready to fly from her lips, beyond her control as he ripped her release from her.

His mouth seized hers.

His long cock drove deep into her in one swift thrust.

Sherry threw her head back and cried out, stars exploding across her eyes and heat sweeping through her as every inch of her trembled and throbbed, bliss crashing over her. She grasped Talon's shoulders, anchoring herself as she flew, afraid she might lose herself if she didn't hold on to something.

If she didn't hold on to him.

His mouth found her throat, his murmured words against it lost on her as her entire body buzzed and tingled.

She fought for air and scrambled to gather her scattered senses.

Talon did that for her.

He seized her hip in his left hand, eased his cock almost all the way out of her and drove back in, deeper this time, until he was in her as much as she could take. She moaned and wrapped her arms around him, clung to him as he rocked his hips, stroking her long and slow, building things up between them again.

She broke through the haze of her first orgasm and shook as she felt her belly heating again, readying for the next.

Shit.

She wasn't sure how much she could take as he stretched her body around his thick cock, touching every part of her, rubbing her in that sweet spot with each deep thrust. She writhed and raised her hips, wanting him deeper still.

He wasn't close enough to her yet.

She needed him to be one with her.

Ached for it.

He moaned and held her. His mouth found hers and she kissed him hard, on the verge of begging him for more. His tongue tangled with hers and he did as she wanted, angling her hips and driving deeper into her, his pace quickening.

She couldn't keep still, lost whatever control she'd had over her body. Need hijacked it. She moved against him, meeting his hips, desperate for more. He grunted and shuddered, dominated her mouth with his tongue as he drove her head into the bed. His right hand clamped down on her shoulder, a hot thrill dancing through her in response, and the fingers of his left hand dug into her hip, holding her fast and stopping her from moving.

She groaned and tried to fight his hold. He tightened it further, pressing short claws into her hips that had her shooting higher, her mind filling with seductive and tempting thoughts about those claws.

About his fangs.

She broke free of his lips, unable to resist the urge that bolted through her, and dragged his head down to her throat. He stilled, his entire body tensing, his hips freezing with his cock buried deep inside her, and then he loosed a dark snarl that had every inch of her shaking in response.

She gasped as his mouth clamped down on her throat and he sucked hard on it before devouring it with kisses, harsh presses of his lips and the blunt edges of his teeth. He started moving again, hips pumping fast and hard, leaving her in no doubt that he felt as desperate as she did, as consumed by his desire and that burning need.

A need that hadn't been satisfied yet.

Her hands ran over his back, the feel of his powerful muscles shifting with each deep plunge of his cock mesmerising her, thrilling her.

Damn, he was strong.

He traced his teeth over her throat, brushed his lips and licked at it, pressing his tongue in hard against her flesh.

Needed more.

She grabbed the nape of his neck.

He grunted and snarled against her throat, thrust deeper and faster, and his mouth clamped down on her flesh.

A low growl rumbled through him, and through every fibre of her being, and he sucked hard on her throat.

Pain mingled with the pleasure, and detonated.

Sherry was fairly certain she screamed at the top of her lungs as her climax suddenly broke over her, the surge of feeling short-circuiting everything and making her ears ring and her entire body quake.

Talon held her down and broke away from her throat, pressed his forehead against it as he thrust harder, faster, his breath washing over her damp skin in swift bursts interspersed with low groans that had her tightening around him, a need to give him a mind-blowing release too seizing hold of her.

He plunged deep and stopped dead, shook in her arms as he growled and grunted, his cock throbbing hard inside her, sending aftershocks of pleasure blasting through her with each one.

She sank into the mattress beneath him, muscles like water beneath her skin as contentment rolled through her, mingling with the warm haze of her climax. Her bones felt too heavy to lift even when she wanted to hold him, needed to have him pressed against her.

He sagged on a sigh, his body coming down to cover hers, and rolled onto his side, taking her with him, keeping them intimately entwined as he continued to pulse.

She slowly opened her eyes and looked into his.

Silence reigned around them, but inside her emotions were raging out of control, stirred to a frenzy by the man staring at her with soft amber eyes that whispered she wasn't alone.

She wasn't the only one who felt this way.

As if she had just lost a piece of herself to him, but had gained a piece of him in return.

As if they were bound together now.

Entwined soul-deep.

CHAPTER 12

Surrendering to his need of Sherry had been dangerous.

Foolish.

It hadn't satisfied that need, it had only intensified it. Now he couldn't get his mind off her, and his primal side, the tiger in him, wouldn't settle unless she was close to him. The pressing need to mate with her, to ensure that she was his, filled his waking hours and invaded his sleep too, manifesting in sultry dreams of her.

Gods, he needed her.

But it had been dangerous.

He had almost lost control when he had been kissing her neck the first time, and had stopped himself from doing something reckless and irreversible by leaving her. The second time?

Talon still wasn't sure how he had resisted biting her.

He had felt her need, the desire that had awoken in her, and he had wanted to satisfy it.

Somehow, he had reined himself in at the last moment, finding the strength to overcome his instincts and settle for sucking on her throat instead.

Not the sort of mark he had wanted to place on her.

Still wanted to place on her.

It was one hell of a mark though, a huge deep bruise that was going to take some time to fade, and was enough to make others aware that she had a male.

That she was his.

In a way.

Talon had expected her to attempt to cover it up, or to be flushed with embarrassment when they had met up with Kyter and the others at Underworld to go over the plan one last time.

Sherry had surprised him by brazenly walking into the nightclub in a low-cut black t-shirt that revealed more than it hid.

Including his mark.

Kyter had spotted it immediately, his golden eyes going dark and questioning her. Whatever look she had given him, it had been answer enough for the jaguar. He had backed off, not saying a word about it to her, or him.

Talon wished he had seen her face.

He wanted to know how she felt.

It plagued him as he paced in the quiet park, surrounded by nature and feeling her comforting touch. He breathed deep, stilled his thoughts and let nature wash over him, carrying away his worries and allowing him to focus again.

Nature had always soothed him like this, had always made him feel connected to something greater than himself, something beautiful and miraculous, and that he wasn't alone.

Byron wasn't bothered about whether he lived surrounded by a concrete city or lush greenery and wilderness. It bothered Talon though and he knew it bothered his other brother and sister.

He didn't like the human cities, even hated the fae towns if he was honest.

This was his home.

The wild green realm of nature.

He purred, letting peace wash over him to carry his troubles away as he thought about the pride village and the lake beyond the forest surrounding it, and his rock, a large flat one that jutted out over the water, standing at least six foot above it. Gods, he loved to sunbathe on it in summer after a swim, staring across the lake to the mountains and the endless blue sky. He had defended it more than once in the early days after the pride had moved there, chasing off the males and making it clear it was his place. They had soon learned to keep away from it, even when he wasn't around.

The image of that place filled his mind, chasing away the city park.

Sherry popped into it, bikini-clad and beautiful as she smiled and waved from the shallows, luring him to her.

Gods, he wanted to take her there.

He wanted her to make it her home too.

With him.

He kept his thoughts on that dream, using it to bolster his heart and give him strength.

It would get him through the next few hours away from her.

Hours that were already testing his strength, pushing him to the limit.

He used the desire to see her again to calm his fear and give him an objective, something tangible that he could work towards, a goal at the end of the dark road that lay ahead of him.

It wouldn't be long now.

He lifted his head and scented the night, trying to discern the hour. It was cold, the heat of day dissipated at last, and the roads were getting quieter.

Soon.

It had to be soon.

His stomach flipped and he breathed through it, trying to expel his fear on each exhale.

Fear that pressed him to turn tail and run before Archangel could find him.

Talon clenched his fists and stood his ground against its assault, refusing to surrender to it. He had to do this. He needed his revenge and had to help the others, but it was bigger than him and it was bigger than them.

The information they found in this raid might help shine a light on a darker side of Archangel.

It might save his species, and the other shifters, fae and immortals by preparing them, making them aware of what the hunter organisation was up to behind the scenes.

That was worth the risk. It was worth reliving a nightmare.

By doing this, he could be helping everyone.

Movement off to his right had him tensing, muscles coiling tight in preparation. This was it. His animal side pushed and fur rippled over his skin. He gritted his teeth and held back the urge to shift, mastering it. It wasn't going to happen.

Not only because he had to hold with tradition.

If he shifted, they were liable to use weapons against him.

Only Emelia was in on the plan, the rest of her group were none the wiser, and therefore an unknown variable he preferred to keep nice and calm, not panicked and on the defensive.

He hunkered down and rubbed at the wound on his side, irritating it with his short claws so it began to bleed again, and smeared the crimson over his stomach. If he looked as if he was already injured, there was a chance he would get through this without anyone shooting him.

The group halted and he focused his senses on them, picked out the female and four males just beyond her. His vision sharpened, the park becoming as bright as day around him, and his fangs lengthened as he called on his primal strength, his true nature.

Better make this look good.

Talon looked over his shoulder at them and bared his fangs in a silent warning to keep away.

Emelia stared at him through impassive green eyes, her face schooled to hide her emotions, a mask of calm and control. While the males at her back had chosen to pair black t-shirts with their black combat trousers and boots, she had opted for a long-sleeved roll-neck sweater. Her deep brown hair had been tied back into an all-business bun.

He kept his breathing slow and steady as he waited, his eyes fixed on her, monitoring her closely as his senses kept tabs on the others.

He wasn't sure how this was going to go down.

Sable had neglected to mention that part.

Emelia slowly moved her left arm, holding it out at her side with her palm facing the others. A warning to stay back?

He glanced at the males, weak creatures, ones he could easily defeat in his current form and would butcher in his tiger one. He turned and rose to stand in one slow fluid motion, coming to face them.

A hiss of air was all the warning he had.

He flinched as a fierce sting pierced the left side of his chest and his eyes leaped there. Numbness swept across his pectoral and over his shoulder, crept down his arm and spread along his stomach. He blinked hard as fogginess invaded his head, slowing his thoughts, and stared at the tiny dart sticking out of his chest, white feathers bright in the slim moonlight.

Fuck.

On a growl, he tore it from his body, and tried to toss it away as he collapsed to his knees. It fell from his lax fingers and he struggled to focus on them, couldn't make them obey him no matter how much he tried moving them. His hand fell to his knee, a weak growl escaping him as that cold numbness continued to spread across his body.

This wasn't how he had imagined it going down.

He roared inside, mad with a need to shift and escape, but no matter how fiercely he battered the cage the drug formed in his body, he couldn't break free of it. He slumped forwards and grunted as his cheek hit the dewy grass, his breath coming faster as panic mingled with the numbness to take hold of him.

It screamed how weak he was, how easily Archangel had overpowered him, and that he was now at their mercy.

And he had no reason to trust them.

He had foolishly expected to be lucid when they took him in, his faculties all in order.

Emelia did another complicated signal and her team broke up, two males circling one way and the others rounding him on the opposite side. She edged towards him, right hand still gripping the damned dart gun she had used on him. He weakly bared his fangs at it as it wobbled in and out of focus.

She twitched it upwards. Once. Twice. A third time.

A signal?

He fought the heaviness in his head and his body and managed to get his eyes off the gun and up to her face. Her lips moved silently, small motions that the others wouldn't see in the slender light.

He frowned, struggling to make out what she was telling him on repeat. Three words. No. Two.

His head turned, and he waited for the darkness to swallow him as it had that awful night all those months ago, the last time he had been exposed to this drug after a long bloody fight and taken into captivity.

He shook that memory away, a pressing need to know what she was telling him as she closed in demanding his focus more.

Two words.

Play.

Dead.

The four males were suddenly on him.

Talon's first instinct was to fight them with all the strength he had left.

He fought it and closed his eyes, gave a pathetic growl and did as the huntress had ordered.

He played dead.

Or at least, unconscious.

But he was aware of them as they shackled his hands behind his back. Aware of them as they hauled him onto his feet, struggling with his dead weight. Aware of them as they dragged him through the park and loaded him into the back of a van.

And aware of the fact the huntress had messed with the dosage of the drug in the dart, only giving him enough to weaken him rather than knock him out.

Maybe she was on his side after all.

He sat quietly with his head hanging forwards, bent over his legs, lolling around as the van manoeuvred through the city streets. Whenever he bumped into one of the males, they huffed and pushed him away. Weak little things. He wanted to snap their necks with his bare hands. Might have given in to that dark urge if his hands hadn't been shackled behind his back.

Talon thought about the others who were waiting for him, and Sherry, using them to keep his head and their plan on track. If he lost it now, chances were he would wake in a cell heavily guarded and the others would be forced to fight when they mounted a rescue, placing them all in danger.

Sherry included.

That was enough to have his tiger side calming down, settling within him. Waiting.

It was a strange unnerving sensation.

He didn't really do patient.

He had been doing it a lot since meeting Sherry.

She was changing him already.

He just hoped it was for the better, and it would help him win her.

The van hit a downwards slope and rounded a corner, and pulled to a halt.

Some fucker had the audacity to slap his left cheek, sending him swaying towards the male on his right. He growled and flicked his eyes open, glaring at the female.

"Good. He can walk himself." She rose onto her feet and removed the dart gun from her thigh holster. "Don't think about getting feisty."

He continued to glare at her.

The males on either side of him grabbed his arms, pulled him onto his bare feet and shoved him towards the rear doors. The other two were waiting on the tarmac. One of the hunters behind him shoved him in the back and he dropped to the parking lot floor, landing silently.

"Think he always lands on his feet?" The male prodded him in his left shoulder, and he obediently walked forwards, fantasising about what he would do to the bastard if his hands had been free, not locked in solid reinforced restraints.

It would be bloody, and beautiful.

Another grinned at him. "We could take him to the roof and find out."

Talon bared his fangs at the bastard and clenched his fists behind his back, his arms tensing as he tried to break the restraints.

"Settle down," Emelia said, and he wasn't sure whether she was speaking to him or her unit. "Since you're all insisting on pissing me off... you can all piss off. Go on. It's past knocking off time."

One of the males, a fair-haired youth who looked as if he had zero experience in the field and would get eaten alive if he crossed a non-human without a team to back him up, looked back at her. "You're sure? I mean... he's a lot of guy to handle alone."

"Are you saying for a woman to handle alone?" Emelia snapped, all warmth leaving her voice. "You want me to write that up in my report, Carter?"

He quickly shook his head.

"Jesus, you're all fucking annoying. Get out of my sight before I write you all up for that little stunt you pulled the other night. I'm sure the higher ups would love to know about you visiting that fae bar to bet on the illegal fights in the basement."

Carter's face blanched. The other three looked as if they might piss in their pants.

Emelia was one fiery little female.

Talon liked her.

The four males hurried into the building ahead of him.

Emelia came up beside him, grabbed his right arm and huffed. "Men. Always doing something stupid and reckless."

Now Talon felt certain she was talking about him.

He glanced down at her.

The troubled edge to her emerald gaze said he might be wrong again, or at least he might not be the only stupid and reckless male she knew.

"Move." Emelia nudged him forwards and he obeyed, trudging through the plain metal door in the concrete wall of the underground parking facility.

She pulled on his arm before he could shoulder the next door open, stopping him in the small space between them. He frowned down at her as she looked around, inspecting all the corners of the ceiling and then closing the door to the car park, shutting them in.

"Hold still." She opened the pocket on her left thigh, pulled out a syringe and tugged the plastic cover off with her teeth. He eyed the needle, every instinct screaming at him to knock it away. He must have tensed, because she paused with it close to his arm and looked up at him. "It's an antidote... but you'll need to act like you're still shaking off the drug."

He nodded and turned, offering his arm.

Stung like a bitch when she stabbed him with it, but the relief was instant, the haze lifting from his mind and strength returning to his body.

Emelia capped the needle again and slipped it back into her pocket. "Sable owes me for this."

And he owed them both.

She pulled down a sharp breath, exhaled it and sucked down another before taking hold of his arm again. He could feel her shaking, but she did well to hide the tremble as she opened the door and pushed him through it. He staggered for effect and weakly growled at a passing pair of humans dressed in white clothing.

"Fucking torturers," he slurred in their direction and they both gave him a wide berth.

"Try to keep it more under control," the male said to Emelia.

She nodded and shoved him again, and Talon wanted to rip the shit out of the bastard with his claws.

It?

Like fuck he was an it. He was more male than that pathetic bastard would ever be.

He shot her a black look. She hit him with one in return and pushed him harder.

"Try to remember who's helping you here, Buddy," she muttered and then in a louder voice added, "Keep moving or I'll hit you again."

He growled and stumbled forwards, finding it hard to play the role of a weak little cub now that his head was clear and his hunger to find the others and deal Archangel a blow was rising, seizing hold of him.

They reached the main cellblock and he staggered to his right, trying to lead the way to the service lift he had used to escape.

Emelia pushed him in that direction, fielding a few questioning looks from several hunters as they passed her by with other prisoners. She glared at them all, her green eyes fierce and full of fire, a dare for them to speak to her. A few of them saluted, revealing the female was above them. He supposed it made sense as they followed the white-washed corridor around a corner. Sable had mentioned Emelia was due to take over her squad.

The little human acted like a pro as she spotted the service lift ahead of them near a branch in the corridor. She struggled with him, pretending he was misbehaving, and shoved him against the wall next to the panel beside the lift doors.

A flicker of nerves showed in her eyes as she pressed the button and waited, keeping a watchful gaze on the people coming and going along the corridor. One of the science types slowed, a female with greying hair.

"You brought him in?" The female looked him over and he had a flashback of her standing outside his cell, watching him for the first few days he had been in their hands.

She had been the one responsible for deciding what course of study he had been subjected to, and had been responsible for all the tests and torture they had inflicted on Jayna.

He snarled at her through his emerging fangs.

"Keep back." Emelia held her palm out in front of her, towards the other human, and pressed her other forearm against his chest. She pushed his back against the wall and held him there, her weight hardly anything, and definitely not enough to restrain him. He played along though. Emelia lowered her hand and reached for her gun. "He's coming around quicker than we expected."

The lift to his left pinged and the doors slid open.

For a heart-stopping moment, Talon thought the scientist would demand to know what Emelia was doing going down the service lift with him, how she knew about the secret facility, and would call others to take both of them into captivity.

The grey-haired female withdrew a small device from her pocket, swiped across the screen several times and then typed something.

When she was done, she looked up at Emelia.

"What are you waiting for? If he's coming around, I want him contained as soon as possible." The female pocketed her device, and relief swept through him, but it lasted only a second. "I've notified the others. We'll be ready to continue our research on him before the hour is up. Well done, Commander Emelia."

No.

He wasn't going back into the cage.

Fur rippled over his skin and he launched forwards, knocking Emelia into the opposite wall. The scientist backed away, narrowly avoiding his fangs as he snapped at her.

"Damn it." Emelia barrelled into him and he grunted as another hiss sounded and cold spread across his left side.

Talon staggered backwards, hit the wall and sagged against it, breathing hard as he fought the drug again and cursed himself for being so stupid and forcing Emelia's hand.

Sound warbled in his ears as the corridor spun, and then he was moving, falling downwards. He shook his head, trying to clear it. The light around him dimmed as he was marched forwards, into a familiar gloom.

The facility.

Voices swam around him as he stumbled forwards, Emelia's hands a constant pressure against his arm and back. Bile rose up his throat as he tried to breathe but kept catching the scent of blood, vomit and bodily fluids.

He couldn't be back here.

He couldn't.

He struggled but Emelia said something, lightly patted his back and guided him onwards, and he thought he caught a word in there.

One that brought light into the darkness of his heart and soothed his primal side.

Sherry.

Talon focused on her, conjuring an image of her in his mind. He could almost feel her, knew that she was close, and that meant the others were close too. He wasn't alone this time. He had been an idiot, had forced Emelia's hand so she'd had to drug him again, but everything would be alright.

He would escape this Hell again.

And this time, he wouldn't be alone.

Familiar scents reached his nose as the gloom brightened to white and his vision started to clear, the fog in his head lifting with it as the remains of the antidote in his system went to work, purging the drug all over again.

The sickening whoosh of a glass panel lifting had his instincts firing again, and he fought Emelia as she pushed him into the white-walled cell he had called home over the last seven or eight months. She jerked on his arms as she unlocked his restraints and then backed off.

His knees gave out as the barrier dropped and he looked over his shoulder at the brunette huntress.

Her green eyes issued an apology and asked him to be patient at the same time.

He slowly dipped his chin, just enough for her to see that he understood and would somehow do as she had asked, but not enough that the people watching the feed from the cameras positioned around the cellblock would pick up on it.

The witch held in the cell opposite him, a diminutive female with platinum hair that faded to black, wearing a dull black dress that had seen better days, came to the front of her cell opposite him.

"Talon, what the hell were you thinking?"

She had an irritating little talent, one that the suppressors installed in the cells couldn't quite negate.

She could read minds.

He shrugged, pushed on to his feet and moved to the glass wall of his cell. "Who said I was thinking at all, Aggy?"

She scowled at him.

It hadn't taken him long to figure out that the way to get her to stop probing his head was to call her Aggy rather than her given name. She always quit poking around his thoughts in exchange for him calling her Agatha instead.

"Your funeral," she muttered and walked over to the right wall of her cell, and gave it a hard kick. "Hey, Grognak… have you seen what cat just got dragged back in?"

The demon mercenary that Agatha had termed Grognak due to her inability to speak the demonic language, something which Talon had repeatedly picked her up on since she hated it when anyone shortened her name, grunted in response and muttered something.

Talon had figured out that his name wasn't Grognak, and that Agatha called him it because she had a problem with demons in general. Most witches residing in the fae towns did, but Agatha's issue with them seemed to run deeper than the usual clash between demons and witches over trade rights and the apparent stealing of business.

He had also discovered in one enlightening conversation that Grognak was a fictional barbarian in a video game.

Agatha apparently preferred playing those to socialising with other witches, all of whom she deemed boring and dull, and lacking the excitement and adventure she craved.

When he had mentioned leaving the fae town and finding some real adventure, she had clammed up and hadn't spoken to him for almost a week. Apparently, leaving home was a definite no for her. He didn't think it was because she lacked the courage either. He had seen her give Archangel hunters and those bastards they employed to torture captives with their studies absolute hell.

Something else was holding her back.

"I might have got caught on purpose. I have a plan." Talon looked both ways along the corridor, and focused on the exit to his left.

Klay, the big shifter in the cell to his right, the one he was sure was a bear, let out a low whistle. "Let's hear it then."

He focused and frowned when he counted only three with his senses. "Where's the wolf?"

Everyone tensed, and he sighed as he hung his head, not needing to hear them say it.

"He went out fighting... after he heard about Jayna... he just flipped when they tried to take him from his cell and attacked them. Managed to kill one of their hunters before they—" Agatha cut herself off.

Talon lifted his eyes, met hers and forced himself to keep looking into them as tears lined her dark lashes and pain shone in their lilac depths.

This was his fault.

He should have come for the others rather than escaping alone.

But what good would he have been to them?

He had been injured, weak from blood loss before he had even made it out of the secret facility. Getting out as quickly as possible had been imperative. He had been in no condition to fight his way through the hunters that would have come down on him if he had lingered long enough for someone to raise the alarm.

They would have had him overpowered and back in the cell in no time, and Jayna's sacrifice would have been for nothing.

The demon said something. Talon liked to think it was complimentary, a sort of 'don't beat yourself up about it', but it might have been derogatory. He only knew a smattering of words in the demon tongue, and he was doubting those since meeting the merc. The male hadn't used any of them, and when Talon had attempted to speak with him, he had simply given Talon a disinterested look and moved off to the other side of his cell where Talon couldn't see him.

"So I hate to break it to you... but you're in a cell again and they've doubled the guard since your escape... I really don't think you're going to be escaping anytime soo—" Agatha fell deathly silent as a roar sounded above them, followed by the muffled grunts of humans.

Talon sharpened his senses, straining to hear through all the layers of stone, steel and wood.

"What's happening?" Klay hissed and he felt the big bear move closer to him.

He shut him out and focused harder, closing his eyes to block out any distractions.

A familiar female voice. Dim, but it was up there.

And it wasn't Emelia.

Another roar. Something broke, several hunters let out garbled cries, and the female shouted again.

Ordering the hunters to back off and hurling an insult at her foe.

A demon apparently.

Talon flicked his eyes open and grinned at Agatha, relief sweeping away all the doubts that had been trying to sink their poisoned teeth into him. "We're getting out of here."

She looked sceptical.

Until the lights suddenly went out, dropping the cellblock into pitch darkness. His eyes rapidly adjusted, revealing Agatha's stunned expression.

Talon looked up to his right, at the camera mounted there, and his grin stretched wider. The red light was off. Someone had disabled it.

"Ready to get out of here?" he said.

"Fuck, yes," Klay muttered, sounding more relieved than Talon felt. "Just tell me I get to rip the bastards a new arsehole on my way out."

Demon merc laughed low at that, a sinister sound that said Klay would have to beat him to each hunter in order to bloody his claws.

This was going to get messy.

A shadowy figure appeared in front of his cell.

Flicked long black hair over her shoulder and curled a lip at the barrier between them.

"You may want to move back a little. Cavanaugh's brother assures me this device has a narrow blast radius but I've never used one before." Iolanthe had twisted the small black disc in her hands and stuck it to the glass wall before he had a chance to distance himself.

She teleported.

Talon hurled himself towards the back of the cell, hunkered down and covered his head with his arms.

The device detonated.

A percussion wave hit him and he grunted as his ears rang and the smell of smoke filled the room. A thousand tiny needles bit into his forearms and shins.

"Fuck," he muttered and gritted his teeth as he emerged and saw all the pieces of glass sticking out of his skin. He plucked one out, tossed it aside and froze. "Agatha!"

He leaped to his feet and was standing in the corridor near her cell a heartbeat later, not feeling the pain in the soles of his bare feet as glass sliced into them. He waved his hand in front of him, clearing the smoke, his heart pounding as he searched for her with his senses and his eyes stinging as he tried to see if she was alright.

Those eyes slowly widened.

She stood in the middle of her cell, her hands stretched out in front of her and a shimmering pale purple-pink bubble surrounding her so she hovered a few inches from the ground.

Completely unharmed.

Her platinum-to-black hair floated around her shoulders as if she was under water and her lilac eyes shone with stardust, twinkling as she maintained the barrier with her magic.

Incredible.

"I think your friends disabled everything," she said in a matter of fact tone and the bubble wobbled and disappeared with a faint pop, and her hair suddenly dropped to land on her shoulders as her feet floated to hit the ground.

He just stared at her. He had seen magic before, but never anything as useful as what she had performed.

Never anything defensive.

She kicked at the glass on the floor of her cell, pushing it aside as she made her way to him. When he didn't stop staring at her in silence, she glared at him.

"Don't give me that look. Now you know why I don't go off looking for adventure. What good would this sort of magic be to me?"

True. If she specialised in magic that protected, she probably had very little experience of magic that was offensive. Attacking spells. Witches normally chose the offensive route, and for good reason. There were a lot of species who didn't like them.

Odd considering those same species would visit a witch in a fae town whenever they required a spell or potion, or lotion for something.

Agatha took hold of his wrists, let her eyelids drop to half-mast and stared blankly at his chest. Her lilac eyes captivated him, distracting him from whatever she was doing as they sparkled, glowing in the darkness.

"Done," she said just as another explosion rocked the cellblock and sent him swaying sideways.

He scowled in its direction, expecting to find Iolanthe there.

Bleu glared right back at him. "You are taking too long. I am not blowing my cover here because you cannot handle a few scratches."

Talon bared his teeth. He wasn't dawdling, and he hadn't asked Agatha to heal him.

Another roar came from above.

"They're making a bit of a show of it," Iolanthe said right beside him and he tensed, his heart leaping into his throat.

She chuckled.

He scowled at her too, because he was damned if she was going to mention how she had got the jump on him. Elves. He was starting to dislike them. It wasn't natural for a creature to just suddenly appear right beside someone. He preferred to be able to track everyone around him, accounting for them all so they couldn't sneak up on him. Elves made that impossible.

"Sable and Thorne always make a bit of a show of it," Bleu muttered. "I've seen them fight enough times. At least Archangel will buy it if it's violent and a little bloody. Thorne is meant to be playing the role of a demon mate intent on bending his female to his will and forcing her away from Archangel in order to pop little demon heirs for him after all."

The way his expression soured at that said that Bleu wasn't in the market for heirs of his own anytime soon.

Talon doubted that Sable was either.

"We get to fight now," Klay growled and Iolanthe looked the big brunet bear up and down.

"No." She laid a hand on him before he could evade her and they both disappeared.

Klay was going to be pissed. Talon had to admit that even he was a little irritated. He had been gearing up to fight his way out of the building again, fantasising about taking out a few Archangel hunters along the way, and maybe seeing if he could get a peek at that room they kept under heavy guard.

Now he had the sinking feeling that escaping was going to be disappointingly easy.

And not at all bloody.

And he wasn't going to get to satisfy his curiosity.

"There's a room near the cage, I want to take a look at it." Talon looked in that direction, and then back at Bleu.

The elf glanced along the corridor. "Are there other captives there? I only took out the power in this area."

Meaning Bleu would have to take it out across the entire secret facility for Talon to get a look at the room beyond that door, and Bleu had made it clear during the meeting at Underworld that using his powers to kill the lights and cameras would be taxing on him.

Talon wanted to nod, just so Bleu would get him that look he wanted, but in the end forced himself to shake his head.

"I could go alone." It was off plan, but the more he stood there thinking about that door, the more he needed to get a look.

"No way. Hunters will spot you, and I am not explaining to Sherry that curiosity got you killed." Bleu huffed as he met his gaze. "Do not give me that look either. I am not helping you. I am sorry, Talon, but I have orders from on high not to expose myself or any elf involvement."

Talon wanted to growl at that, but drew down a deep breath and crushed that urge, somehow found the strength to shake off his curiosity and let it go. Bleu was right. Escaping took priority, as did keeping the hunters unaware of what was happening. Hopefully Sherry and Emelia would find some information that explained what was beyond the door.

Bleu took hold of Agatha, who merely stared at him in abject fascination. "Are you really an elf?" she said as they disappeared.

Iolanthe reappeared. "I'd better make this quick. We made Kyter stay on the roof to protect it and he's just figured out it was a trick to keep him out of trouble."

She grabbed the demon and teleported.

Leaving him alone.

For five seconds, the amount of time it took for Bleu to reappear and grab him.

A shiver went down his spine, lighting up his senses.

Sherry.

"Wait," he snapped.

The elf paused and arched a black eyebrow at him. "If this is about that damned room again—"

"No... I need to find her... I need..." Talon interjected, his senses reaching out and searching for her. She was in the building now. He could feel that much. He just wasn't sure where.

How far away was she?

Was she safe?

He needed to see her.

"You need to get to the roof." Bleu's grip on his wrist tightened, and then relaxed a notch as he sighed. "It will be risky... the lights are still on in the main building... but I can go."

Talon wanted to say yes to that, to beg him to do it, but he forced himself to shake his head. He couldn't ask the elf to risk exposing his people to Archangel, not when he had been kind enough to rescue him and his friends. The male's hand was trembling against Talon's wrist, and he could feel that he was weakening, that teleporting and using his psychic abilities to cut out the power to the secret facility had taken its toll on him.

After teleporting Talon to the roof and the others, Bleu probably wouldn't have the strength left to both cut the power on the floor where Sherry was and teleport in and then out with her.

He would expose himself to Archangel, going against his orders and placing his species at risk of retaliation from the hunter organisation.

No. As much as he wanted Sherry safe in his arms, he couldn't ask the elf to do it. He needed to think about the bigger picture, about keeping Archangel in the dark for as long as possible, unaware that the shifters, elves, demons and fae had been warned they were up to something.

"Just take me to the roof," he said and Bleu nodded.

As darkness swept around him, Talon clung to the thread that connected him to Sherry, linking their hearts and telling him that she was safe right now.

She was strong.

Brave.

He had to trust that she could do this. He had to believe in that strength and her courage.

But if he felt a change in her emotions, even the slightest trickle of fear, then he was going back in.

They landed on the roof of the elegant sandstone building, in a shadowy corner behind a rumbling air-conditioning outlet. He glanced down into the courtyard far below, tracking the hunters moving around it, unaware of him and his friends, and what they had just done.

And what they were about to do.

His gaze shifted to the door across the roof from him.

He stared at it, his heart beginning a slow pound as he willed Sherry to hurry, to get all the information she could on Archangel and get out of there.

His limbs twitched, his animal side prowling just beneath his skin as he waited, losing patience, and he started pacing, desperately trying to work off some energy and give his tiger some release. Kyter's steady gaze tracked him, filled with sympathy that said the jaguar knew what he was feeling, how he was slowly going crazy and it wouldn't be long before he lost his grip on his primal instinct to protect Sherry.

When that happened, he wouldn't be able to stop himself.

He would shift and hunt her down.

He would go back into the lion's den for her.

Even though he knew he wouldn't come back out.

CHAPTER 13

Sherry kept her nerves in check as she casually walked along the corridor on the second floor of the Archangel building, Emelia at her side. The pretty brunette had met her at the roof access door and brought her down to this level shortly after Thorne had shown up to cause a ruckus in the cafeteria as planned.

By the sounds echoing through the building, and the occasional rush of armed hunters past her, Sable and Thorne were still fighting.

She looked down at her boots, trying to see beyond the wooden floor to the lowest level of the building.

Was Talon still down there?

Emelia had explained that she'd had to put him in a cell to make it look good after she had run into one of the scientists in charge of whatever went on down there, but that Bleu and Iolanthe had been given his location and were already on their way to rescue him and the others.

The huntress had been silent ever since, lost in her own thoughts as they headed towards the central archive.

Sherry offered a flirty smile to a hunter who glanced her way, distracting him as he frowned at her as if he was trying to place her. It worked. He grinned right back at her and went on his way, only pausing to look back at her before entering one of the offices that came off the corridor.

She tried to focus on Talon, needing to know he was safe and convinced she would be able to feel him in the way he said that he could feel her. A way he had implied ran deeper than simply him feeling her on his sharp senses. She felt stupid when she felt nothing, an idiot for even trying.

"Not far now," Emelia said in a low voice.

Sherry's nerves instantly rose, trying to get the better of her. She breathed slowly to calm her racing heart and tamped them down, telling herself on repeat that she would be fine and no one would suspect her. Apparently hunters visited the archive all the time, checking the files for information on their latest target.

The people in there would just think she was another hunter researching a mark.

She slipped her hand into her right pocket and felt the USB drive there, turning it in her fingers. It was one she had found in her apartment.

One she was going to use to download Talon's file.

What secret was he trying to protect?

If she asked him, would he tell her?

Emelia slowed.

Sherry stopped and looked back at her, frowned as the woman stared straight through her, her eyes wide and lips parted. Spacing out?

"What's wrong?" Sherry closed the distance between them and Emelia snapped back to her.

"Nothing." Emelia hesitated in a way that screamed it was something. "I'm just a bit on edge."

"Because of what we're doing?" she whispered.

The brunette shook her head.

"No." Emelia paused again, looked at her as if she was trying to pull her apart and see how she ticked, and then sighed and glanced off to her right, to a window there that opened onto a courtyard. "Someone I know... I think he's done something stupid... something that might get him killed. I'm worried about him."

That made two of them.

Sherry didn't want to probe, because she hated it when people poked around in her private business, but Emelia looked as if she needed to talk to someone and get it off her chest.

"What do you think he's done?"

Emelia's green eyes slipped shut. "I think he went to Hell... to hunt a dragon for me."

Wow. Whoever he was, he was definitely in love with Emelia. No doubt about that.

And suicidal.

Dragons were ridiculously strong from what she had heard, and the men working at Archangel didn't exactly look capable of hunting one. She eyed one as he passed her—a regular human man. Not strong enough to take down a sixty-foot shifter with teeth that were probably almost as big as her.

Unless Emelia's man wasn't human.

"Is he a hunter here?" Sherry edged a little closer still, aware that people were looking at them as they passed and sure that if the man in question wasn't one of them, Emelia would get into trouble if they heard about her mysterious and non-human lover.

The huntress shook her head again.

"Is he strong?" Sherry watched her face closely, but not as closely as she watched the people coming and going along the corridor.

Emelia was helping her. She was damned if she was going to expose her and whatever was happening between her and this man.

Emelia nodded.

"Capable of killing a dragon?

Another nod.

"So you're just worried about him because you feel something for him?" She could relate to that. She was worried about Talon too, even though she was sure he could take care of himself and Bleu had probably teleported him out of the building by now.

"No." Emelia's eyes met hers. "You don't understand... like dragons aren't meant to come here... he isn't supposed to go there."

Sherry knew enough about dragons after meeting Loke to know what Emelia was getting at, and why she was worried.

Dragons were stripped of their powers and died if they dared to leave Hell. Loke had been in a bad shape when the elves had brought him to Underworld, close to dying, and he had only been away from Hell for a few days at most.

Emelia believed the man she loved was about to suffer the same painful fate, but in reverse. He was going to die because he had chosen to enter Hell, to fight a dragon for her.

"Is there nothing you can do?" Sherry's chest ached for Emelia when her dark eyebrows furrowed and she shook her head.

A huge boom rocked the floor and Emelia's green eyes shot down to her feet.

They widened and then narrowed.

"Maybe there is something I can do after all."

Something that terrified her, but something she was going to do regardless if the steely look in her eyes was anything to go by.

Sherry had the feeling that Thorne was going to be taking more than one huntress back to Hell with him.

An alarm sounded and she almost jumped out of her skin. Damn it. She covered her ears, flinching at the high pitch wail, and squinted as red lights flashed, hurting her eyes.

"Is it that fucking demon again?" someone yelled.

Hunters streamed past her, heading for the stairs that led downwards, and Emelia grabbed her wrist, tugging her in the opposite direction.

"Now," the huntress said and she hurried to keep up with her, a sense of urgency suddenly flooding her as they raced along the corridor.

They skidded around a bend, almost ploughing straight into two men. One shouted that they were going the wrong way.

Emelia didn't slow, and Sherry could see why as she dragged her eyes away from the hunters and focused on running again.

Ahead of her, twin doors loomed at the end of the corridor, and the sign above them read 'Central Archive'.

They were here.

The doors burst open as they reached them, a woman coming out of them with a blade at the ready. Sherry plastered herself against the wall to avoid being cut and then ducked into the room the moment she had passed.

Emelia released her and headed straight for one of the computers on the long double rows of desks that filled the middle of the room. All around the edges, huge black cases lined the white walls, the servers stacked in them flashing with green, orange and red lights.

Sherry grabbed the computer opposite Emelia so the huntress couldn't see what she was doing. Her hands shook as she took out the two USB drives, one from each pocket. She pushed the first into the slot in the black tower beside the flat screen, and woke the display with the mouse.

A pale blue screen came up with a column of links down the left side and Archangel's winged logo in the centre of the space on the right, just above a search box.

She typed in the names Talon had given her one by one and moved those files onto the USB drive. All of the files contained a link to a page that documented the raid on the fae town. She quickly skimmed it, frowning as she realised it was just one raid in many, something Archangel were doing with increasing regularity to track down different species for their research.

Thankfully, the file contained links to all the profiles of the captives, so she was able to track down the demon they had taken with Talon. Her frown increased as she read the demon's notes and saw everything they had put him through, gruelling tests that had lasted hours, and invasive procedures designed to not only uncover how his biology worked, but how quickly he could heal major wounds.

The bastards had left him open on the table, had forced him to deal with his own wounds when he had come around, all so they could document his regenerative abilities.

An urge to head out into the corridor and punch the hell out of the hunters in retaliation blasted through her.

"I don't like what I'm reading here," Emelia said, stealing her focus. The brunette lifted her gaze to her over the top of the monitors that separated them, her emerald eyes cold and hard, but lit with fire. "What the fuck are they up to?"

Sherry wanted the answer to that question herself. Archangel were meant to protect innocent non-humans, but they were experimenting on them in secret, learning everything about them, including their weaknesses.

Were Archangel about to do a one-eighty back to the days when they had hunted and killed any non-humans?

What had prompted them to do such a thing?

She scrolled through the list of raids and stopped when she hit a date where they went from one every few weeks to almost one every other day. Why the sudden spike? Her eyes widened as she looked at the date when the increase had started.

It was only six months ago.

A shiver tripped down her spine.

She clicked on the first raid and her blood ran cold as her worst fears were confirmed in the very first sentence.

It is proposed in the aftermath of discovering the existence of another plane that Archangel must broaden its knowledge of all non-human species through any means necessary and forge forwards towards ensuring the safety of mankind.

Archangel had learned of Hell.

Someone in the organisation had seen it as an opportunity to steer Archangel towards a more violent future under the banner of protecting mankind.

Sons of bitches.

The non-humans rarely bothered her kind, had co-existed peacefully with them for centuries now according to her friends, and she seriously doubted everyone in Hell was a threat to mankind. They were just living their lives, in their own world, far away from this one.

Hell, the elves had moved their entire species there thousands of years ago because her world had become too violent for them.

She needed more information.

Some of the profiles of those captured with Talon contained links to projects, so she clicked all of those too and saved all the related documents, following the trail deeper into Archangel's heart.

She kept hitting an encrypted file at the end of each path, one that required high level clearance and several passwords.

Project Abaddon.

Sherry tried to move the files for it over without decrypting them but the system refused, stating that without access she couldn't retrieve the documents.

She could move some related files though, ones that mentioned it. Hopefully that would be enough for them to piece together what Archangel were up to.

Another rumbling roar echoed through the building.

She hurried to find the next file, aware that Sable and Thorne wouldn't be able to keep fighting much longer and would have to get out. The plan had been for a fifteen minute argument in the cafeteria and then Thorne would win and steal Sable away.

It had to be close to time now.

Sherry tracked back to the search page and typed in Talon's name. She did her best to grab the file and put it on the second USB drive without looking at it, but the first line below his name caught her eye. It stated he was a tiger shifter, which was nothing new to her. The estimated age based on his appearance and other factors including a blood test was though.

Three to four hundred.

Here she was pushing thirty-six, and he was potentially pushing four hundred.

She closed the file and deleted it off the servers, and did the same with the other ones.

Just one more to go.

She typed in another name and opened the file. A picture of a beautiful woman filled the rectangular panel on the left of the screen, next to her name.

Jayna.

They listed her as only two to three hundred, and her height and weight. She read down the page, her stomach slowly twisting as she found she had been subjected to experiment after experiment for over twenty different projects, far more than the others. One stood out, a project name unfamiliar to her, and she clicked on it to download it.

Froze with her eyes locked on the first line.

They had tried to force her to breed with Talon, drugging her to rouse a need to mate. Sickness brewed in Sherry's stomach and she told herself not to read on, but she couldn't stop her eyes from devouring each line, even when she feared what she would find.

Talon had been brought to her several times over the period they had been in captivity.

On the last occasion, they had drugged him too.

The result.

She couldn't look, didn't want to know if he had slept with another woman, wasn't sure she could bear it if he had, even though they hadn't known each other then.

She moved the mouse to the close button on the file and paused with her finger hovering over it.

No.

She needed to know, because if she didn't look, it would eat away at her, and she didn't want anything coming between them. She didn't want to end up driving him away because she was unsure of this one thing about him, and unable to control her emotions, believing he had gone through with it.

She steeled herself, lowered her eyes from the corner of the page and read the last line.

It was two words.

Experiment failed.

She let out her breath and deleted the file without downloading it, sure Talon wouldn't want to be reminded of what they had put him and Jayna through, and wouldn't want the others knowing about it.

She clicked back to Jayna's file and reached the notes at the bottom.

Her heart dropped through her feet.

It was a location followed by the word 'authorised' and today's date.

A shiver ran down her spine and thighs.

Jayna had given them the location of a pride.

Talon's pride.

Archangel had dispatched a team there.

CHAPTER 14

Talon couldn't describe the relief that blasted through him as the roof access door finally opened and Sherry came rushing out of it. He was across the flat roof as quickly as he could manage, tearing up the distance between them and sweeping her into his arms before she had even noticed him. She gasped, struck his chest as he hauled her up against him, and then melted into him when his mouth found hers and she realised who he was.

Her hands slipped over his bare shoulders and up the nape of his neck, and he growled low into her mouth as he kissed her, a thousand hot tiny shivers dancing down his spine in response to her caress.

A little moan escaped her, teasing his ears and stirring thoughts of carrying her away into the deeper shadows.

She suddenly pressed her hands to his shoulders and broke away from his lips, and he growled and tried to seize them again, unwilling to give them up when he needed her fiercely, had been going out of his fucking mind waiting for her to show up and show him she was safe.

"Talon." Her soft delicate voice was so serious that he stopped trying to kiss her and lifted his eyes to hers. They held a grim edge, one that sent a different sort of shiver down his spine.

Did she know about his secret?

His heart started a thunderous beat against his chest, his palms sweating where they pressed against her backside, holding her off the ground and against him.

She swallowed hard, glanced at the others as they came to meet them, and then looked back into his eyes.

"Archangel... I'm sure it was a moment of weakness... that she just wanted whatever relief they promised..."

He didn't like the sound of that. "What?"

Her sombre expression and the fear he could feel trickling through their link had his emotions switching from worry she had discovered the truth about him, to fear she had discovered something terrible about someone else.

Somewhere else.

They couldn't have.

"Not the pride," he whispered, his throat so tight that he barely squeezed out the words.

"There's still time. They only dispatched a team today."

"Bleu." He set Sherry down and turned to the elf.

The dark male stood like a wraith in the darkness, his violet eyes cold and deadly. "Whatever you need, you will have it."

"I need to reach the pride. I can tell you a nearby portal."

Bleu nodded. "It will be enough."

"I'm coming too." Kyter shoved his fingers hard through his sandy hair, positively growling the words, and Talon nodded, because he wasn't about to turn the jaguar down. His kind were strong, warriors to the core after everything they had been through, and Talon would need his fighting talent if he was going to protect the pride.

Most of the tigers there weren't warriors. They were females, and children. Easy targets for Archangel hunters.

"*We're* coming too," Iolanthe corrected her mate and stepped up beside him.

While Talon didn't want to turn her down, he had a problem with her accompanying them. "If you come... the others. I need them safe."

They weren't free of Archangel yet.

He looked at Agatha where she stood beside Klay, half his size. The bear could fight. Talon had seen him take down three Archangel hunters the night they had been snatched from the fae town. But Talon knew the male would be distracted with protecting Agatha. Bears were territorial about any female, highly protective. Klay and Agatha had bonded during their time in the cells, sharing the same dry humour and exchanging tales.

Although, Agatha told him tales of the video games she played, and he told her stories of his real-life adventures and brushes with death.

"Not a problem," Bleu said and before Talon could ask what he was going to do, fearing he meant to teleport the others away from the rooftop to somewhere safe, draining himself and risking not being able to teleport him to the pride, the elf turned to the demon mercenary and spoke in his tongue.

Whatever he was saying, the demon didn't look particularly pleased about it. Reluctance shone in his near black eyes, a corona of purple-red shimmering around the edges of his pupils, a sign his emotions were getting the better of him.

The male said something back at the elf, and glanced at Agatha. Tore his gaze away. Glanced again.

His black horns flared, curling around the lobes of his ears.

Aggression.

Talon hadn't realised that the male felt such a thing towards Agatha. Had she pushed the demon too far with her silly name for him? Demons could be a ridiculously proud race.

The huge black-haired demon took hold of Klay's arm, and reached for Agatha. He hesitated, his fingers flexing in the air between him and the witch. On a growl, he seized her arm, and they all dropped into a black hole in the ground that closed behind them.

"He agreed to take them back to the fae town." Bleu turned to him.

Thank the gods. He could focus now, wouldn't have any distractions when he reached the pride and would be able to fight with a clear mind.

Or at least he hoped he would be able to.

"I don't like how the demon's horns flared with aggression." He looked back at the spot where they had disappeared, a ripple of worry running through his blood. If the bastard hurt Agatha, Talon would hunt him down.

Bleu cocked an eyebrow. "Aggression? Believe me, the last thing Valdaine is feeling towards the little witch is aggression."

If it wasn't aggression, what was it?

The answer hit him like a tonne of bricks.

Oh.

Talon wasn't sure which to be more shocked by—the fact that he knew the demon's name now, or the fact the male wanted Agatha.

He had the feeling that adventure was about to come and bang down her door.

He would have to warn her once his pride was safe. A huge obstacle still stood between him and achieving that.

Bleu and Iolanthe could only teleport directly to somewhere they had visited before. The elves had to rely on using the fae portals dotted around the world to access somewhere new to them.

"The nearest portal is in Ullapool... but it's a long way from the village on Tèarmann." Close to fifty miles in fact, and Talon wasn't sure Bleu would have the strength to teleport him to Ullapool and then onwards, leaping short distances to the furthest point he could see until they reached the pride village.

Bleu's violet eyes lit up. "Kincaid's estate?"

The elf knew the old werewolf? Fuck, he was glad to hear that.

He nodded. "He gave us refuge on a section of his estate to the south west, away from his home... separated by a lake and a mountain."

Talon hoped that was enough to keep Kincaid safe from Archangel. The werewolf had done a lot for his pride, and he didn't want him and his family being dragged into this mess.

"South entrance, Io." Bleu took hold of him and Sherry as Iolanthe nodded, and had teleported them before Talon could say she wasn't coming.

The elf landed hard in a dark forest, immediately released them and dropped to his knees on the leaf litter.

Iolanthe and Kyter appeared a split-second behind them, and the female rushed to Bleu the moment she spotted him on his knees. "Brother!"

Shit. Talon couldn't exactly ask Bleu to take Sherry home now. Even Iolanthe was showing signs of fatigue, her fair brow dotted with sweat.

"Quit fussing," Bleu muttered as he grabbed her shoulder and pulled himself onto his feet. He swayed a little as he brushed his knees down but managed to remain on his feet. "Stupid tiger is stronger than he looks. I didn't expect that sort of drain."

He swatted her hands away when she tried to keep hold of him.

"I'll be fine." Bleu succeeded in brushing her off him.

Mostly because she planted her hands on her hips and glared at him, her face darkening to reveal just how much she doubted that.

"Ah, leave him be. You know you can't stop him when he wants to do something." Kyter weathered the black look Iolanthe threw over her shoulder at him. "Look, he's already back to being annoying."

The female elf fixed her focus back on her brother as he produced a long black blade out of the air and swept his hand along it.

The damned thing turned into a spear.

Talon really had a lot to learn about elves.

"This isn't your fight," he said and both of the elves turned murderous glares on him. He held his hands up at his side. "I'm just saying. You have orders not to reveal the involvement of elves in what happened. If any of the hunters from Archangel see you—"

Bleu smiled coldly, flashing sharp fangs. "Oh, they won't see me."

Damn. As much Talon wanted to turn him down, he also didn't want to get on the elf's bad side, and he needed all the help he could get. If the male wanted to bloody his blade a little, Talon wasn't going to stand in his way.

Iolanthe drew a short black blade from the air, and then produced a longer silver one. She tossed it to Kyter, who caught it in one hand, and grinned at her.

"Is this an order not to go all jaguar? You just don't want the lady tigers seeing me in all my glory."

She huffed at that.

By 'all my glory', Talon figured he meant naked and not in his feline form. Female tigers wouldn't be interested in a jaguar, but they were drawn to warriors, their instincts pinning them as viable strong mates. A naked Kyter would probably draw some unwanted attention from them.

Iolanthe teleported another shorter silver blade into her hand, walked over to Sherry and held it out to her. The female elf nodded when Sherry took it, her violet eyes flashing with confidence and strength that she imbued into Sherry with only a handful of words.

"Stick them with the pointy end."

Sherry nodded, flexed her fingers around the bound leather hilt of the sword, and took a deep breath.

His stomach lurched at the sight of her swinging the blade, and the thought of what was about to happen, and every instinct he possessed had him stepping towards her, driven to stop her.

"You don't have to do this. You could stay here." Where it was safe. Where Talon wanted her to be, far away from the fight.

She shook her head, determination shining in her blue eyes. "Not going to happen. I've had my share of training. Besides, I have the best back up in the business."

Kyter growled low at that.

Like hell Sherry was talking about him.

Although Talon did appreciate that the male would be keeping tabs on her too. Not that Talon intended to let her out of his sight, or away from his side.

"Got one of those for me?" He turned to Iolanthe.

"I thought you would go all tiger… but if you want a weapon." She held her hand out in front of her and a huge broadsword appeared in it. "I figure you can handle this."

Hell, yes, he could.

He took the weapon from her, growled as he felt the weight of it and gave it a few test swings. Damn. It was a nice blade. Made for cutting down anyone who stood in his path.

He would use it well.

"This way." He pointed in the direction of the pride village with the sword.

Bleu, Iolanthe and Kyter took off, leaving him alone with Sherry.

He swept her into his arms and claimed her lips, needing to feel them against his, needing to taste her and know that she was with him, and to thank her for wanting to fight for his pride.

She smiled against his lips. "Let's go do this."

He caught the hidden meaning in her words—and then they could have some much-needed alone time.

He was up for that.

Pride first, pleasure later.

"Hold on." He didn't give her much of a chance to do that as he kicked off, leaving her shocked gasp somewhere back in the woods.

She wrapped her arms and legs around him and clung to him as he raced through the forest with her. Gods, she felt good all pressed against him like that, clinging to him. He banded his free arm around her and held on to her too.

He would never let her go.

The lights of the village flickered through the thick trees ahead of him in the valley.

The scent of blood hit him before the screams reached his ears, and the roars of the warriors as they fought.

He growled low in his throat, his fangs elongating as rage poured through him, fury that Archangel had dared to bring this fight to his doorstep and were attacking innocent members of his pride, females and children who couldn't defend themselves.

He sprinted harder, determined to reach the village and end the battle.

Determined to save his people.

A mighty roar sounded, sending the birds flying from their roosts above him.

A shiver danced over his arms and down his back.

Grey.

His younger brother.

He pushed himself to the limit, adrenaline pumping now and his instincts seizing control. His senses honed, sharpening until he could feel every single person ahead of him and could almost pick them all out one by one.

Another roar answered the first.

Unmistakable.

Byron.

A garbled scream followed it, one of the Archangel team if the sudden spike in the scent of mortal blood in the cool night air was anything to go by.

Talon shifted Sherry slightly away from him to protect her hearing.

Unleashed a roar of his own to answer his brothers.

To let them know he was coming and he wasn't alone.

He broke into the clearing where the village stood.

Stopped dead as his gaze tracked the first Archangel hunter he spotted and saw their target fighting another, the naked silver-haired male stood with his back to them as he battled the mortal with his bare hands, utterly unaware they were poised to strike.

"Grey!"

CHAPTER 15

Talon released Sherry at the edge of the clearing in the forest and was gone in a flash. She swung around, heart pounding at a sickening pace against her ribs and adrenaline flooding her body, making her shake so hard the sword she gripped in her right hand rattled.

Everywhere she looked, people were locked in combat, the black-clad hunters of Archangel wielding swords and crossbows with deadly expertise while Talon's pride fought with their bare hands.

Or as tigers.

Several of the large gold-and-black cats thundered past her, heading towards a group of Archangel hunters who were breaking cover at the far right of the village. The leader pounced, landing with his huge paws on the shoulders of one of the hunters and his hind legs ploughing into the man's stomach. The tiger's head came down, huge fangs bared, and Sherry flinched away, unable to watch as the shifter claimed the hunter's neck.

A horrific scream rose above the din of battle and a cold shiver skated down her spine.

She shouldn't be here.

This wasn't her place.

She was mortal, untrained in combat, weak and vulnerable.

Dressed like the damned hunters who wanted to hurt the tigers.

A deep roar resonated through the village of wooden cabins and her gaze swung towards the source of it, fear of dying morphing into fear of witnessing the owner of that beautiful roar suffering that fate.

Talon launched at the back of a hunter, his broadsword gripped in both hands, held low at his left side. When he reached the man, he brought the sword up in a devastating arc, slicing straight across the hunter's back. The man unleashed a roar of his own, filled with pain and fear, and went down hard. Talon didn't stop. He leaped over the man, grabbed a large naked guy by the nape of his neck, and pulled the male behind him as he thrust forwards with his blade.

It punctured the side of another Archangel hunter, sending the man staggering backwards and then slumping down into a heap on the dirt.

"Godsdammit!" Talon turned on the silver-haired male, his amber eyes bright and wild as he came to face him, running over every inch of him. She could almost feel his relief when he saw the male was unharmed, although he didn't show it. He shoved the male's shoulder, forcing him to plant one bare foot behind him to stop himself from being tipped off balance. "Fucking be more careful."

"Love you too, Brother." The silver-haired shifter gave Talon the finger and pushed him away with his other hand. "I had that. You know I did. You always have to push in and take over. Always have to be top tiger. You've been like it since birth."

Talon huffed and glanced her way, scrubbed a hand around the back of his neck in a way that told her how awkward he felt about her hearing this. Why?

The male's piercing ice-blue eyes shifted to her. "Byron is going to love this."

"Fuck off, Grey," Talon snapped, flashing fangs. "I save your arse and all you can give me is lip?"

Grey growled, baring his own white daggers.

The two stared at each other in silence.

Sherry began to feel a little awkward herself.

Not because of the way they were behaving, but because she was starting to feel as if she was staring into a strange sort of mirror as she looked at them, one that reflected certain aspects of Talon but reversed others.

Grey was almost identical to him.

Only his silver hair and blue eyes set them apart.

They were more than brothers.

They were twins.

Talon cracked first.

He grinned, grabbed Grey by the nape of his neck and dragged him into a hug. "Fuck... I thought I'd never see you again."

Grey resisted for all of a second before he was wrapping his arms around his brother and squeezing him tightly while slapping his back. "You know I wouldn't let that happen. I'd just about convinced Byron to let me look for you. Knew some shit was up. Something just felt off. Still does."

Those piercing blue eyes slid her way.

Talon pulled back and frowned at his twin. "Nothing's off here."

It wasn't? Or was it? She wasn't sure, wished she knew what the hell they were talking about in code, because it was certainly about her.

Her eyes widened as two Archangel hunters came rushing from beyond a cabin to the right of them.

"Talon!"

He spotted them before she had even started to scream his name, turning on a pinhead to block the sword one of the men swung at him.

Grey had shifted before she could catch up with what was happening and pounced on the hunter on the left, taking him down and savaging his chest with his claws as he ravaged the man's throat with his fangs.

Sherry stared at him, fascination sweeping through her to make her forget the battle that raged around them.

The huge tiger lifted his head, frosty blue eyes swinging her way, and bared his fangs at her on a hiss, his fur stained with blood around his mouth and on his paws.

He was beautiful.

White and black.

Not a drop of amber on him.

And he was gone before she could gather herself, sprinting into the fray again, tackling a huntress as she went for one of the women frantically trying to usher two children to safety.

Talon jogged back to Sherry. "Sorry... he tends to react like that the first time someone sees him."

Because he was different, and he probably felt it more keenly than any tiger because his twin had come out normal, fur a striking shade of deep gold and black.

She shook her head, and smiled when Talon took her hand, pressing his thumb against her palm. He stared at them, a myriad of emotions sweeping across his face, all too brief for her to catch and decipher.

When he lifted his golden eyes to hers, they were sombre and distant. "I didn't want you here."

She stepped closer to him, settled her hand on his bare chest, over the tiger inked on his left pectoral, and looked up into his eyes. "I know... but I want to be here."

With him.

She didn't want him to face this alone, or Byron once this battle was done. She wanted to be there for him.

"Come on." He tugged on her hand and she ran with him, skirting the edge of the battle.

A fire raged to the right of the village now, one of the smaller cabins ablaze, the flames reaching high to dance in the darkness, releasing bursts of sparks as a gentle breeze blew and caught them.

Bastards.

Why was Archangel doing this?

Fire swept through her blood too, igniting it and rousing her courage. That courage rose higher as she glanced off to her left and saw a huge jaguar savagely battling two Archangel hunters who had cornered another woman.

Kyter was fighting.

She looked just beyond him as the air there shimmered and Bleu suddenly appeared, his spear making swift work of one of the hunters for Kyter, earning him a low growl of disapproval. Iolanthe finished up with a huntress and crossed the distance between her and her mate in a heartbeat, appearing between him and Bleu.

"No... we are meant to be fighting Archangel, not each other." She fixed Bleu with a withering glare, which he returned one-hundred-fold. The guy knew how to make his feelings clear with just a look, she had to give him that. Iolanthe turned that glare on her mate. "Shoo... go help the others."

Kyter grunted and loped off, joining a pack of tigers as they prowled through the throng of hunters and shifters.

"This way." Talon tugged her towards the burning cabin. "We need to see if anyone is in there."

Sherry followed, heart thundering wildly, making her dizzy as she scanned her surroundings, fearing someone would get the jump on her. Another team of Archangel hunters broke out of the forest to her right and Talon snarled, released her and leaped into action.

Hell.

He had been made for war.

She skidded to a halt near the blazing house, stunned by how swiftly he moved, how graceful he appeared as he ducked and dodged, and swung the broadsword as if it weighed nothing, as if it was all a dance, perfectly choreographed and practiced a thousand times. He cut down two hunters with one swing, twisted and stabbed a third in his thigh, crippling him.

The fourth aimed a crossbow at his back and Sherry reacted without thinking, all of her fear and the battle drifting away in an instant as she launched towards him and raised her sword. The man turned towards her, his crossbow swinging with him, and she brought her blade down hard in a diagonal arc.

The hunter's finger pressed against the trigger.

Her sword sliced down his left shoulder and across his chest.

The tinny odour of blood flooded the air and her stomach rebelled.

The hunter grunted and collapsed to his knees, the crossbow falling from his hands as he looked down at the blade sticking out of his stomach, pointed towards her.

Talon's blade.

Her warrior tiger stood behind the man, his amber eyes cold as he stared down at the back of his head and twisted the sword, ripping a shriek from the hunter. He pressed his bare foot against the male's back and kicked forwards, drawing his sword back at the same time and pulling it free.

The man groaned and landed on his side.

Sherry continued to stare at him, at the blood that pooled beneath him and coated the edge of her silver sword.

She hadn't killed him, but she had wanted to.

She felt numb.

"Sherry," Talon barked and approached her slowly.

Odd.

He looked worried, as if she was about to fall apart.

His amber eyes dropped.

Hers fell too.

Landed on the slim wooden bolt sticking out of her thigh.

What?

She blinked, mind fraying, unable to process what she was seeing as a dark slick patch crept down the front of her black fatigues.

"Gods," Talon growled and eased onto his knees in front of her.

He tipped his head back, eyes seeking hers, searching them.

For permission.

She nodded slowly, closed her eyes and steeled herself, aware of what he was going to do and that when it happened, the pleasant numbness she was enjoying would be obliterated by pain.

"I'm sorry," he whispered.

All the warning she had.

She screamed as white-hot pain blazed over her thigh and burrowed into her hip bone, so fierce she turned away and vomited. Darkness swept over her but strong arms held her, anchored her to the world together with his deep voice as it murmured in her ear, telling her how strong she was and how brave, and whispering other things to her through those words, things that told her of his heart, and echoed what was in her own.

Sherry sank against him, using his strength, taking all that she could from him because she refused to pass out. Not here. Not now. His pride were still in danger, and if she lost consciousness, he would be too. She knew it deep in her heart. She would be a distraction, and she wouldn't be able to live with herself if that got him killed.

"Talon!" A soft female voice rose above the growls and grunts surrounding her.

Talon shifted against her, and she wearily opened her eyes and looked at him. Her vision wobbled, the pain flowing through her still so intense that it stole her breath. His handsome face lightened, filling with concern as he looked off to his right.

Sherry followed his gaze, blinked to clear her vision, and stared at the beautiful woman running towards them, her deep gold dress whipping around her long legs and a small white bag bouncing around in her left hand.

A vicious hiss sounded in her ears again, and she tried to shoo it away, didn't want to listen to it because she was bone-deep tired of being jealous of every beautiful woman who knew Talon.

She didn't want to be that way anymore, didn't want to feel threatened by every stunning female who so much as looked at him, all because they belonged with him more than she ever could.

Because they were all immortals.

Tigers.

"Maya," Talon snapped, darkness falling like a shadow across his face as his black eyebrows dipped low, narrowing his amber eyes. "What the hell are you doing outside?"

Maya looked over her shoulder as she stopped in front of him, her long black hair falling down the left side of her chest and her amber eyes seeking something. The place where she was meant to be?

Why did Talon want her away from the fight?

To protect her?

Sherry looked up at him as he held her in his arms, still kneeling on the floor with her, clutching her close to him.

Yet she felt she was drifting away, or was that him?

She could see the love in his eyes as he looked at this woman, the deep affection, and it made her realise he had never looked at her that way. There had been desire, lust, and maybe affection, but not love.

This was the way he looked at someone he loved.

Sherry tried to push out of his arms, but he huffed and clucked his tongue at her, and held her even closer, crushing her to him. When she kept shoving at his chest, he heaved a long sigh, and looked from her to the woman, and back again.

"This is Maya… my reckless sister who is meant to be in the main cabin with the other females and children." Talon gave her a pointed look. "I'm assuming Byron issued that order?"

Maya's cheeks pinkened, and then her eyes flashed fiercely. "I can fight."

Talon huffed. "I don't have time to argue with you. Go back."

"No." The slender shifter stood her ground, but her hands shook as she held them at her sides and Sherry could see the fear building inside her, recognised it because it was building in her again too. "I saw her hurt… I wanted to help."

He huffed again. "Fine."

Before Sherry could protest, Talon had hauled her onto her feet and into his arms, lifting her like some damned weak princess.

"I can still fight." She pressed her hands against his shoulders and fought another sickening wave of pain that spread outwards from her thigh, hoping he wouldn't see it.

His amber eyes slid her way. "Not you too."

He couldn't have sounded more exasperated if he had tried.

A roar echoed around the woods.

"Byron," Talon hissed and looked ahead of them, all the irritation leaving his eyes, swiftly replaced with worry.

Sherry looked towards the centre of the village.

Ten hunters fought there, surrounding a single large tiger.

The animal hissed and swiped at them, forcing them to dodge backwards to avoid its claws, but they were closing in, preparing to strike.

"Go," Sherry whispered and looked back at Talon. "He needs you."

He swallowed hard and looked down at her, and her heart ached. He had never looked so torn, so afraid, as if she was asking him to do the impossible by leaving her yet he felt the pressing need to go.

She cupped his cheek with her left hand. "Go. Maya will take care of me."

Talon glanced at his sister. She nodded. His face contorted in a vicious grimace and he growled through his teeth as he looked from Sherry to Byron and back again.

His brother needed him, and he was wasting time.

She was going to make this decision for him, because he wouldn't be able to live with himself if something happened to his brother, and she would never forgive herself either.

She shoved hard, pushed right out of his arms and landed on the dirt with a spine-jolting thud that had her biting back a cry as fresh pain rolled through her.

"Go!" she snapped when he still dawdled, staring down at her.

"You dare get hurt," he bit out, deep voice a growl of thunder, and then he was gone.

Maya beamed at her. "He *really* likes you."

He did?

She looked at Maya for an answer to that question, but the black-haired tigress was focused on her white bag, pulling bandages from it in a long stream and cursing as they got tangled.

Sherry tracked Talon as he barrelled into the group of hunters, only realising as he grabbed one and hurled him away from Byron that he was bare handed, his sword forgotten. Panic began to creep and curl through her as he fought, knocking the arms and wrists of any hunter with a sword to stop them from landing their attacks.

He needed a weapon.

Or to shift.

Byron was fighting in his tiger form, Grey beside him now, both majestic and vicious tigers. Why wasn't Talon joining them?

"Shift, dammit," she muttered.

Maya paused and looked over at the fight, her voice laced with a sombre edge. "Oh, Talon."

What the hell was that supposed to mean?

Before she could ask, Maya looked back at her, golden eyes awash with sorrow.

"He has a thing about tradition... when... how long has it been since he escaped and Jayna died?"

Sherry wracked her brain. "Two... maybe three days."

"Not long enough. He's mourning Jayna... he can't shift yet."

But Byron had shifted, and Jayna had been intended for him. Wasn't he mourning her too? Did Byron care about her at all?

"It's a stupid tradition," Sherry grumbled and grunted as she moved onto her knees and then slowly rose onto her feet, ignoring Maya as she tried to stop her.

Damn, her leg hurt like a bitch. She put weight on it but fire screamed up her body and she barely stopped herself from crying out.

Sword.

She had to get the sword to Talon.

She wasn't strong enough right now to carry his broadsword, so she plucked her smaller blade from the dirt.

"Get out of here," she said, but Maya didn't move. She looked at her, caught the concern in her eyes as she watched Talon, and Talon alone. She didn't fear for her other brothers, because they were strong as tigers, swift and taking down hunters together. Talon was fighting alone, four on one, and with only his hands as weapons. Sherry placed her hand on Maya's shoulder and gently squeezed, and Maya glanced at her. "Go. I'll make sure he's okay. I really like him too."

Maya managed a smile and nodded, and then she was gone, ducking past Iolanthe and Bleu where they were taking down the last of a group near the largest cabin and disappearing inside.

Sherry clutched the blade and hobbled towards the centre of the village, her focus locked on Talon. She moved as quickly as she could, most of the hunters uninterested in fighting her because she was dressed like them and the tigers thinking twice the moment they neared her.

Could they smell Talon on her?

"Talon," she whispered, heart screaming across the distance between them that she was coming.

A shockwave of heat rolled over her and she swiftly turned to her left and staggered backwards, away from the nearest cabin as fire exploded from the front door and the small window, and licked up along the porch.

The anger that had begun to blaze inside her earlier when Archangel had set the first cabin alight to flush out the women and children burned hotter.

It became an inferno of fury as she spotted two male hunters and a female pulling three women from the next cabin along, and a fourth hunter outside it with a canister of gasoline.

Bastards.

A dark-haired and very naked man came out of nowhere and sliced the huntresses throat with his claws, freeing one of the women, and took on a hunter next, causing him to lose his grip on another. She ran straight towards Sherry.

The hunter with the canister looked her way, and his eyes narrowed as he spotted her. "You... I saw you with one of them. Traitor! She's working with them."

Sherry's blood turned to ice.

Someone roared.

Everything slowed.

He dropped the canister, turning at the same time, bringing his other hand up as the third hunter shoved the last woman away from him and reached for his hip.

Both drew guns and had them aimed in an instant, one directly at Sherry and the other at the running woman as she passed her.

Her heart missed a beat as both guns fired, a flash of light the only warning she had as her ears rang and she stared death in the face.

A wall of darkness came down across her vision and she flinched away, heard a scream she thought might have been her own and smelled blood, thick and strong, choking her.

Male screams joined hers, the scent of blood growing stronger, and then the sound of boots pounding the dirt. Wind whipped past her, something jostled her, and someone growled.

When silence fell, and she could breathe again, awareness of the world gradually came back, little by little.

Someone was holding her.

Someone who smelled like Heaven.

Sherry burrowed into him, wanting to be closer still, afraid she was about to lose him, because this was the end for her.

Wasn't it?

"I want a fucking word with you," someone snarled.

With her?

Talon moved back, a pained hiss leaving him. "Later."

"Now," the man barked. "You fail to protect my future bride, lead Archangel to our pride, and then you insult me further by proving yourself incapable of protecting one of my current brides?"

She cracked her eyes open and they widened when she saw the woman sprawled on the ground near her, her eyes sightlessly staring at her and a dark patch covering her back.

Naked masculine legs filled the space just beyond her, and Sherry tracked them upwards, to their owner's face.

The black-haired male scowled down at her, eyes like fire in the low light.

He sneered at Talon. "You certainly managed to protect your mate though."

Mate?

Talon swallowed hard as she looked at him, but he refused to look at her, kept his profile to her and his eyes fixed on his brother.

Those eyes slowly closed and he hung his head. "It's true. I failed Jayna... and I failed Alicia... and I did choose to protect my fated one over her..." He lifted his head and fixed hard eyes back on his brother, and bit out, "But tell me you wouldn't have done the same thing if our positions had been reversed."

Hell.

It was Sherry's turn to swallow hard as her mouth dried out.

She was Talon's fated one?

Working with Kyter and Cavanaugh had told her everything she needed to know about this particular aspect of shifter life. They could fall in love with anyone, but they all had a single fated mate, one they felt was made for them and with whom they could have a deep and powerful bond. She was human though. Sure, she felt connected to him, deeply drawn to him, but being his fated one? It seemed so impossible.

Byron looked as if he might strike Talon for saying that, and then all the tension left his wide shoulders and he eased back a step.

"It doesn't excuse what you did." Byron's amber eyes lost only a drop of their iciness and his tone remained as frigid as the Antarctic. "You led them here."

"Jayna led them here," Sherry blurted and flinched away when his cold eyes dropped to her.

Talon growled, and she had the feeling it had been a warning to his brother because Byron shifted his eyes away from her. "It's true. Jayna told Archangel our location. I didn't know, or I would have come here sooner."

"You should have come home straight away."

Sherry wasn't going to sit still and let him speak to Talon like that, treating him as if he had done everything wrong when he knew nothing about what had happened. "Talon couldn't... Archangel were hunting him, and he was severely injured."

"She's telling the truth," Kyter put in as he tugged on his trousers and buttoned them, seemingly oblivious to the black looks all the tigers gave him.

Or ignoring them.

Iolanthe stood at his side, cleaning her black blade and watching everyone closely, making it clear that if anyone dared to attack her mate just because he was a jaguar and not a tiger, she was going to skewer them.

Sherry would be right there with her.

Bleu too.

He hadn't taken his violet eyes off Byron the entire time he had been speaking with Talon.

"Talon came to my nightclub for sanctuary," Kyter said. "Sherry took him somewhere safe so he could heal."

"Once he was strong enough, we infiltrated Archangel." Sherry needed that one out there, because no damn way she was going to let Byron get away with not knowing just how much effort all of them had put into protecting the tigers and all the immortal species. "We got all the information we could and that's when we found out Archangel knew this location. As soon as I told Talon, we teleported here."

Byron looked down at Talon.

"It's true. We have to move." The solemn edge to Talon's deep voice, and the way his eyes drifted around their burning village, made Sherry want to hold him until his pain ebbed away and he found his strength again.

They had won the fight against Archangel, had left none of the hunters alive by the looks of things, but they had lost tigers in the process, and their home.

Byron growled. "I decide when we move. Not you."

Talon didn't react to that. She felt a tremor run through him, swore she could feel a flicker of his emotions, his hurt, and she wanted to lash out at

Byron and retaliate for him. She did her best to bite her tongue for his sake, aware it would only make the situation worse.

And in a way, she couldn't blame Byron for being angry.

Or any of the tigers that surrounded her, licking their wounds, tending to each other, and to the dead.

Archangel had attacked them, and Byron wanted to lash out at someone, needed to blame someone after their home had been violated and their pride members killed.

By humans.

Sherry became increasingly aware of the tigers that surrounded her, a wall of men hemming her and Talon, and her friends, in against one of the cabins.

She became increasingly aware that she was human too, the only human left in the village now, and she was dressed like an Archangel hunter.

Talon curled his arm around her waist and pulled her closer, as if he had felt her rising fear and had sensed the air shift, growing darker around them. His eyes didn't leave his brother's, held them calmly, a steely edge to his and the set of his jaw. His fingers flexed against her, muscles coiling in readiness as he waited for Byron to make a move.

Byron stared him down.

Raised his hand.

Talon tensed.

Byron growled.

"Move it. We're leaving, and we're leaving tonight."

The group surrounding her splintered, everyone rushing into action, and the darkness lifted, drawing all of her fear out of her. She sagged against Talon and drew slow breaths to steady her pounding heart.

Byron continued to stare down at Talon, silent so long she began to feel nervous again. A need grew inside her, a fierce desire to take hold of him and shake him until he said what was on his mind. She needed to know, because she feared it was something about her, and something that was going to hurt her.

He glanced at the other tigers as they hurried around the village, and then looked back at Talon and softly said, "We're leaving... you know what that means?"

"I do," Talon husked, his voice steady, filled with certainty that had those damned nerves rising swifter, flooding her head with painful images she didn't want to see but couldn't shut out.

His brother huffed, pivoted on his heel and walked away.

Sherry looked at Talon, not following. Why was Byron upset? Shouldn't she be the one upset about what was going to happen? Talon refused to look at her. His eyes remained locked on his brother's back.

Byron stopped a short distance away, and looked back over his shoulder. "Someday... if she makes the leap... they'll be ready then."

She still didn't understand, but whatever was happening, it had gravity to it, weight that settled on her chest and pressed down on her.

Iolanthe, Kyter and Bleu muttered something about Kincaid and disappeared, leaving her alone with Talon.

Alone, but hurting.

Unsure, yet afraid.

"You're leaving?" she whispered, and he finally looked at her. Her heart broke a little as his eyes said that he was, that she was the one who should be upset and not Byron, but she held it together, clutching the fractured pieces and refusing to let it fall apart.

Refusing to let herself fall apart.

Until he gently cupped her cheek, tilted her head up so their eyes met, and lowered his lips towards hers, and whispered against them, "I'm leaving with you."

She really didn't understand now. "Your pride—"

"The pride will still be a part of me... and I will still be a part of it... but right now... many of them will find it hard to trust humans."

Humans like her.

Wait. Did that mean he wanted her to be with him?

"What I did," he started, sighed and tipped his head back, staring up at the stars as if they could guide him or give him strength. He lowered his head again, meeting her gaze once more. "You are my fated one... but it wasn't the reason I chose to protect you over... it isn't the reason I put you first."

His eyes told her the things he couldn't find the courage to say, shone with the love he held in his heart for her, revealing it to her at last.

She felt it too, that quickening of the pulse, that warming of her heart whenever she looked at him and he looked at her. It was more than desire. It was deeper than that.

Deeper than love.

Her gut whispered to her, telling her that she was Talon's fated one and it didn't matter that she was human. They were destined, made for each other. Soul mates. This time love would work out just fine, and it wouldn't be messy and painful, it would be wonderful.

All she had to do was give it a chance.

Give Talon a chance.

She just had to take that leap Byron had mentioned.

Whatever the hell that was.

Talon smoothed his fingers across her brow, distracting her before she could ask about it, and brushed them down her right cheek, his eyes holding hers. "It's going to take a while before they're ready."

"Ready for what?"

"Ready to accept you," he murmured and rubbed his thumb across her lower lip, making it tingle and sending a shiver of heat over her skin.

He gathered her closer.

Hissed.

She quickly pushed back and ran her eyes over him, charting all the wounds that littered his chest. None of them looked deep.

"Don't fuss," he said in a voice that made it clear she was going to fuss whether he commanded it or not. "It's just a little hole."

A hole?

Her eyes widened.

"Fuck... the bullet." She had forgotten about the bullet that had been aiming for her.

A bullet that he had blocked.

A bullet he had taken for her.

"It'll heal." He swatted her hands away when she tried to get him to turn around so she could see his back and the wound. "Let me finish."

He sounded so serious that she stopped trying to see and stilled, her eyes leaping back to his, that strange gravity pressing down on her again.

"When a tiger finds his mate... she becomes his home... she becomes his pride in part... a new pride... made up of just him and his mate. You're my pride now, and my home is wherever you are... so one day... if you're ready and you step into my world... and into the pride born of my blood, then it will become my home again. Fuck, this isn't coming out right. I never figured I would have to make this speech." He looked beautifully irritated, confused and afraid at the same time.

"Why not?" She frowned at him. "Because it's rare for tigers to find their fated one?"

He shook his head.

"Byron said something about making the leap... and now you're talking about me stepping into your world... but feline shifters... I know a few things, Talon, and I know cat shifters can't turn people... you're all born as shifters... but I'm confused because you sound as if you're not talking about me joining the pride as a human." Her voice shook and she cursed her nerves and how much this was affecting her, tearing her apart inside as she tried to figure everything out. She wanted to be with Talon, but how was that even possible? Unless. "If we mated... would I become immortal like humans do when they mate with demons or elves?"

He looked away, sighed and solemnly shook his head.

Sorrow arrowed through her, stronger than she had ever felt it, ripping into her as she thought about that and the fact she would only have a short time with Talon even if she did take the leap and they mated, that she would continue to age while he remained the same. She had foolishly started to dream of a life with him, one where they could be together forever, like Iolanthe and Kyter, and Cavanaugh and Eloise. She had wanted that for them. Maybe this love was fated to be messy and painful after all and her gut was wrong.

Talon quietly turned to face her.

Sucked down a deep breath.
Rocked her entire world on its axis.
"If we mated… you would become a tiger."

CHAPTER 16

Twenty-three days, nineteen hours, forty-one minutes and seventeen seconds had passed since Talon had told his secret to someone for the first and last time.

He paced the deserted village, working off some energy, trying to keep his head and his heart from twisting him in knots as he waited.

She would come.

He had risked everything for her, had told her the one thing he had felt sure would drive her away forever and could have ended up damning his pride.

He hadn't been able to stop himself though.

The need to make Sherry his mate had been too fierce, was still too strong, easily stealing control of him and driving out all sense and reason, leaving him mastered by his feelings.

He had sworn to give her a choice.

He wouldn't have been able to live with himself if he had made her believe that nothing bad would happen if they mated and he bound them together with his bite.

It would have destroyed him.

So he had told her his secret.

Gods, she had been shocked. Whenever he closed his eyes, he saw her pretty mouth opening in a startled O and her blue eyes widening, filling with feelings that had ranged from surprise to fear, and everything in between.

He liked to hope there had been a lot of love mingled in there too.

And that there still was.

He hoped she trusted him as deeply as he trusted her.

Loved him as deeply as he loved her.

Sherry had been silent as he had confessed everything, had bared the part of him he had been warned to keep hidden at all costs, risking it all.

He wasn't just a tiger.

Somewhere way back in his family tree, one of his ancestors had cross-bred with another shifter species to bring added strength to their bloodline and place them in a position of power within tiger society.

The species of feline shifter they had chosen to mate with was the strongest, born of the fires of another realm, both dangerous and beautiful.

And the only species that could turn people.

Hellcats.

With each generation, the effects were growing weaker, but he and his siblings still had enough hellcat blood in their genes to make them stronger than normal tigers, and able to turn others with their bite.

Talon turned and strode towards the woods, kicking his boots off as he went. He lost his shirt somewhere along the way too, leaving it behind in the forest, his feet carrying him along the path as his thoughts flowed like a torrent, pulling him towards the lake.

Had she changed her mind?

He lifted his head, dragged night air over his teeth and tried to scent her. Nothing.

She had changed her mind.

He rubbed the centre of his bare chest, trying to ease the ache building there. He had to trust her. She had said she would come.

It had been her idea.

But gods, she had looked so afraid when he had mentioned hellcat blood, had brought up some damned human hunter who had been turned by one and had almost died.

Talon had been filled with a need to reassure her, to gather her into his arms and tell her he would never let that happen to her, that he couldn't lose her and would rather not mate with her than put her through something that might kill her.

She had stopped him just before his hands had reached her, halting him with a handful of words.

Four wonderful ones.

It wouldn't stop me.

Fuck, he had switched places with her in that moment, staring at her and reeling from the shock that had rushed through him, his head spinning as he had tried to take it in and believe he had heard her right.

Double fuck, but she had never looked more beautiful than she had in that moment when he had asked her whether it really wouldn't stop her from becoming his mate, and she had stood up to him, all determination and fire, and set him straight.

Her words would be branded on his mind, and his heart forever.

What they had was real. Fast but real. She felt that deep down, in her heart.

When he had asked whether she would really go through with it for him, she had hit him with a response that fitted her so perfectly.

She had said she would do it for herself, because she didn't want just a few years with him.

He had told her that she had all the time in the world to make her decision, which had been the toughest fucking thing he had ever had to say because he needed her as his mate, felt as if he was going to lose his mind if it didn't happen soon.

It was going to happen.

He scented the air again.

She would come.

It had been her idea after all.

Two nights ago, in a back room of Underworld, she had told him she was ready.

At first, he had figured she was about to climax, but she had made it startlingly clear she meant something else, something world-changing for them both.

She wanted to be his mate.

Fuck, it had taken all of his willpower to stop himself from sealing the deal right then and there.

Somehow, he had found the strength to stop himself and to give her time to think it over, because they both needed to be sure, and if he had gone through with it then, he would have been haunted by the thought she had merely been caught up in the heat of the moment.

So he had given her time.

Two torturous days in which he had stayed away from her, living at the pride's old village, waiting for her to show up.

He charted the position of the moon, grunted when he realised it was visible now, skimming the tops of the mountains as it rose full and beautiful.

She was late.

He paced the shoreline, desperately trying to pull his shit together.

She would show.

He shoved his fingers through his black hair, clawing it back and tugging on it. She *would* show.

He stopped dead, cold racing through him.

What if she didn't?

He pivoted on his heel, a need to return to his car and drive all the way back to London blasting through him. He made it three steps before he pulled on the reins and stopped himself. He had sworn he would give her time.

Shit, if she needed two years, ten or twenty, he would give them to her.

This was a monumental decision for her.

He knew in his heart that she wouldn't die from his bite, because he had seen his aunt go through the process. She had been mortal, turned in secret by his uncle against the wishes of the pride's alpha at the time, Talon's father and his uncle's brother. When his father had discovered what had happened, his uncle had been punished, outlawed from the pride. Talon had often wondered whether it had hurt his uncle, and whether he would have chosen not to turn her if he had known doing so would see him kicked from the pride. Before meeting Sherry, he had thought his uncle would have chosen the pride over her. Now, he knew his uncle had chosen the right path.

Even if Byron had told him he would lose his place in the pride, would no longer be welcome there, he still would have chosen to turn Sherry and claim her as his mate.

She would survive this, and she would become like him, and they would be together forever.

But it was going to hurt like a bitch for her.

Pain wasn't the only problem. It would alter her too, change her entire life, and it was going to take a lot for her to adapt to that. It was going to be hard on her.

But he would be there for her, with her, every step of the way.

Whether those steps started tonight, or in two decades.

Talon began pacing again, the soft sandy soil at the water's edge cool beneath his feet as he followed the curve of the lake. The air was still, silent save the occasional distant hoot of an owl and the breeze playing through the trees.

Gods.

Where was she?

He couldn't take much more of this, was going to go insane if she kept him waiting. His pacing quickened, his muscles twitching beneath his skin as he struggled to keep his breathing level and even. Measured. A growl curled up his throat, the restless feeling growing inside him, becoming stronger as he turned to pace back the other way and saw the moon was higher. Time was slipping past.

His teeth ached, gums tingling as his fangs elongated, and he flashed them at the night, his mood degenerating as the thought she wasn't going to come taunted him.

Tortured him.

He had given her time, and she had changed her mind.

He had let her slip through his fingers.

Talon threw his head back and roared at the starlit sky, unleashing all the fear, pain and panic in one long silence-shattering bellow. It did nothing to calm his mood, or quell his need to shift.

He had to run.

He needed to run until his bones ached, his muscles trembled, and he passed out from the exertion.

He stripped his trousers off, kicked them aside, and growled through clenched teeth as fur rippled over his skin and the familiar burn began in the marrow of his bones.

Pain ricocheted through him, brief but sweet, making him feel alive as his body transformed and he fell to all fours on the soft dirt. He snarled and shook his head, fire sweeping over his skull as his nose flattened, jaw shifted, and brow widened. His ears moved upwards, rounded and grew. His fingers dug into the dirt as their bones shortened and flesh deepened, growing around them. Fur covered them and rushed up his arms as they followed his hands' transformation into paws. He snarled as his legs shifted and his spine stretched, his ribs altering and sending a deeper sort of fire through him.

His tail was always the last to come, springing from the base of his spine like a whip to lash at the night.

Talon lowered his head, breathing hard through the transition, waiting for the pain to fade.

A scent hit him.

Vanilla and honey.

A shiver washed over his skin and he threw his head back and roared again, a triumphant one this time that he felt all the way to his soul.

Sherry.

He kicked off, racing into the forest at top speed and then instantly slowing as his nature stole control, the desire to see his female again rousing an instinct to stalk her, to hunt her and claim victory over her.

To make her belong to him.

He prowled through the dark woods, slinking between each tree with his head held low, each step careful and slow, making no sound that would give him away.

The scent grew stronger as he neared the village, mingled with another familiar one. The female elf. He stilled and focused, barely resisted the urge to growl when he sensed only one female ahead of him, heard only one trembling heartbeat that spoke of nerves.

Talon hunkered down, moving low to the ground as he stalked her through the trees, using his senses to track her.

As he moved out from behind a thick pine trunk, he spotted her.

His breath left him in a rush.

His heart kicked hard against his chest.

Gods, every inch of him was aware of how beautiful she was as she stood bathed in moonlight on the track to the lake, her golden hair down around her shoulders and a silver low-cut top and black jeans hugging her curvy figure.

Mine.

He stalked her as she started to walk, illuminating her path with a flashlight, and watched her from the shadows as her blue eyes darted around, a hint of fear in them as she kept a close eye on the trees.

Could she feel him hunting her?

Was she aware a predator watched her?

Wanted her?

Another growl rolled up his throat and was held back somehow.

A burn started low in his belly and warmed his chest, a need that he knew he would never be able to shake when it came to her.

To his mate.

He moved around so he was behind her, silently broke cover and stepped out onto the track.

She stopped the second he did, her shoulders tensing, but then she did the most amazing thing.

And he fell even deeper in love with her.

Those shoulders relaxed, her hands falling to her sides, and she slowly turned to bestow a smile upon him so dazzling it stole his breath.

"You pissed at me for making you wait?" she said, all light and grace, not a trace of fear in her as she faced him.

Saw him as a tiger for the first time and recognised him.

"Or just enjoying hunting me?" she whispered, voice a low and throaty purr that made that burn in his belly grow hotter.

Fiercer.

The bond between them was already strong if she could feel that the tiger standing before her was him, could recognise him in this form, and they hadn't even mated yet.

He bared his fangs at her, drew down her scent and growled at the thought of her being his mate, hungry for it to happen because he had felt as if a piece of him had been missing since the day he had met her, a piece that he knew would return when they bonded.

He would feel complete at last.

Her smile held, fucking grew wider if he was being honest, and she braved a step towards him. Her head canted, causing her fall of golden hair to skim across her right breast.

When she reached him, she eased down into a crouch right in front of him, so close he could feel her heat on his fur. He watched her silently, struggling to hold himself back when he wanted to pounce on her, aware that he needed to give her control.

Let everything be her choice.

Her hand lifted, and sweet fucking gods, he purred like a damn cub when she gently cupped his left ear and stroked it, running her palm over it. His hind legs weakened when she pushed her fingers through the thick fur on his cheek and rubbed the spot below his ear.

Talon couldn't stop himself from rubbing against that hand, needed to mark her with his scent so the whole world would know this incredible woman belonged to him, and he belonged to her.

"I'm sorry I made you wait," she whispered softly. "I thought it would be funny."

He didn't.

He shifted back, tearing a startled gasp from her as she fell backwards, landing on her backside and sending the flashlight spinning and rolling towards the woods.

Talon crawled forwards, forcing her down against the dirt and covering her, holding himself above her on his fists.

"I thought I was going to go mad... thinking you wouldn't come," he growled each word, showed her all the pain and hid nothing, so she would know just how much he loved and needed her. "I thought I would never see you again."

The light in her eyes faded, and her smile slipped away. "I didn't think about that. Sorry."

She touched his cheek, and damn, it was bliss, Heaven to him.

Her hand slipped around the back of his neck and she adjusted his idea of Heaven.

She lured him down to her. Welcomed him. Wanted him.

He dropped to his elbows and seized her mouth, kissed her so hard he feared he would hurt her but he couldn't hold back, needed this contact with her, desperate to feel she was there with him and desperate to be hers.

She looped her arms around his neck, drew him closer and arched against him, rubbing her clothed body against his bare one.

Fuck, he needed her naked, needed to be inside her, and needed to claim her as his mate.

He sucked down a breath and forced himself to break away from her mouth, to back off and do this right, before they both got swept up in the moment.

Sherry gazed up at him, lips swollen from his kiss, eyes heavy with desire, her golden hair spread across the dirt and moonlight washing the colour from her skin.

"You're sure?" he murmured, part of him not wanting to ask her that because he feared her answer, feared that she might have come here tonight to tell him it wasn't going to happen yet and he would have to keep waiting.

She stole his heart when she nodded.

"It's going to hurt." He was a fucking idiot for continuing, for giving her chances to change her mind, but he couldn't stop himself, had to be sure.

He didn't want her regretting tonight.

He wanted it to be wonderful for them both, something they both wanted and would look back on in centuries to come with fondness and joy.

This was going to be the start of their new life, one they would share together.

It had to be wonderful.

He would fucking make sure of that.

"It's not going to be easy... I'm not going to paint you a pretty picture, Sherry... I'm not going to lie to you. It's going to hurt, and it's going to be hard for you..."

She pressed her palm against his cheek, her eyes sincere but shining with determination, stealing his breath as they held his. "But you'll be there with me, won't you, Talon? I know you. You won't let me go through this alone. You'll be there through it all... for me."

He nodded, closed his eyes and pressed a deep kiss to her palm. "Every step. I won't be away from you for a second. I'll be around so much... fussing over you... that you'll want me out of your sight."

He slowly opened his eyes and looked down into hers.

They smiled at him. His heart beat a little harder.

Nerves sent his limbs trembling.

He pulled his shit together again and held her gaze, needing to see the answer in her eyes as well as hear it from her lips.

"You'll be my mate then?"

He had asked her that question twenty-three days, twenty-one hours, fourteen minutes and nine seconds ago.

Her answer?

One day.

Was that day today?

Sherry linked her hands behind his head and smiled up at him as she lured him back down to her and whispered two words that he was going to record forever together with that look so he would always remember this moment.

"I will."

Talon dropped his head and captured her lips again. Her kiss seared him as she clutched him to her, a desperate and wild thing in his arms, her actions conveying the impatience that ran through him too.

Gods, she was strong.

Beautiful.

She was taking a tremendous leap to be with him, and it humbled him.

He deepened the kiss, slowed it down despite her attempts to keep it fast and fierce, needing this moment to be perfect. She finally gentled her kiss, sweeping her lips across his, light brushes that had him on the verge of floating in her arms.

Her body arched against his as she moved, and he groaned into her mouth as she wrapped her legs around his waist, hooking her booted feet against his bare backside.

Her little moan as she brought his hard shaft down into contact with her and rubbed against it, maddening him with the friction of her clothing and the need she ignited to be against her flesh-to-flesh, almost undid him.

He rolled onto his back, taking her with him, and tugged at the hem of her top, pulling it up her back.

She broke the kiss and rose off him, tugging off the top and tossing it away from her.

Talon swallowed hard at the sight of her bare breasts, her nipples dark in the moonlight, beaded and calling to him.

He grabbed her around the waist and tried to pull her down to him, but she twisted free of his grip and leaped off him. He growled at her, but she didn't come back.

She stared off into the distance, along the path she had been taking when he had made his presence known.

"Is that a lake?"

Before he could say that it was, she took off towards it.

Talon rolled onto his knees and groaned.

Sherry bounced along the path ahead of him, stripping off her boots and her jeans as she went.

His groan became a growl when she revealed she wasn't wearing any underwear.

Damn. He had never seen a backside as beautiful as hers.

He loosed a low snarl and sprang to his feet, launching after her. She looked over her shoulder, squeaked when she saw him sprinting towards her, and quickened her pace.

She wouldn't be fast enough to evade him until she was a tiger.

Fuck, she was going to be beautiful.

She was going to drive him wild.

He was never going to be able to get enough of her.

He grabbed her from behind just before her right foot hit the water and she laughed as he hauled her up into the air and twisted her in his arms to face him. Her whole face glowed with it, with happiness that looked as foreign to her as it was to him.

One hand came down on his shoulder and the other ploughed through his black hair, slender fingers tugging on it as she pulled his head back. Her mouth claimed his, her kiss fierce again, dominating him in a way he found he loved. He had been in a position of power his entire life, had never submitted to anyone, not even Byron.

He willingly submitted to her.

Her tongue duelled with his, stoking a dangerous need inside him, a dark urge to make her submit to him, to show her just how powerful he was and that he was the only male she needed.

The only one for her.

He growled and seized control of the kiss, and his reward was the sweetest moan he had ever heard.

Gods, his fangs itched, body felt too tight, as if he would explode if he didn't claim her soon.

He needed to claim her, before she changed her mind, before she could escape him. She had been made for him. She was his everything.

He wanted to be her everything too.

He angled his head and kissed her deeper, sank to his knees at the water's edge and groaned as her legs parted and slid down his hips, and her warm core met his aching shaft.

It throbbed against her, as eager for her as the rest of him, sending pulses through him that were both pleasure and pain, a sweet torture that he endured as he kissed her. She rubbed against him, rocking her slick heat along his cock, and he groaned again, his breath coming faster in short bursts as he struggled for control.

Her nails scored his shoulders, spurring him on.

He growled and dropped his lips to her throat, devoured every inch of it and nipped at it with his teeth as he grasped her backside and drew her closer, pressed her harder against his shaft. Part of him had hoped it would stop her from driving him mad with the rubbing, but it only encouraged her, only worsened the torture as she rocked on him, breathless little moans leaving her lips and teasing his cheek.

"Talon," she murmured, a throaty plea that sent a shiver tumbling down his spine and cranked his need higher at the same time as it unleashed the side of him he had been trying to keep under control.

He growled against her skin, his fangs pressed against it, his entire body as tight as a bowstring as he fought to master the urge, the driving need.

Sherry made that impossible.

She rose off him, reached between them, and stroked his cock, easing it down through her slick folds.

Talon roared and had her twisted in his arms in a flash, her back pressed against his chest. She cried out as he drove her down onto his cock, sinking deep into her, trembling deliciously in his arms. He wrapped his arms around her, cupped her breasts and toyed with her nipples as he fought for control again, tried to claw back some semblance of it anyway. He was beyond being in control now, could only hope to hold himself back enough that he didn't hurt her.

She moaned and rolled her hips, and he shuddered and groaned, pressed his teeth against her shoulder as she tormented him. Her hands came down on his, stroking over them, and then dropped lower, caressing his thighs between hers and then reaching back to run over his hips. She sighed as she lifted her arms and stroked up the back of his head, and held his mouth against her flesh in a way that told him everything.

She did want this.

She welcomed it, needed it as fiercely as he did.

She was ready to become his mate.

He lowered his right hand to the curve of her waist and twisted her hair into his left. She moaned as he pulled on it, tugging her head back, and began moving on him, slow and deep, pushing him to the very brink.

Talon slowly thrust into her, as deep as she could take him, drinking her moans as she arched and tightened her grip on his head, holding on to him. Heat curled in his belly, became a fire that blazed out of control before he could stop it, and he slid his hand up and cupped her breast again, tweaked her nipple and tore another moan from her as he began to quicken his pace, driving harder, deeper still, filling her with every inch of his cock.

She rolled her hips, rotating them in a way that had his heart pounding harder, that brink coming at him faster. She pushed him closer still by lowering one hand and stroking it between her thighs, brushing his cock with her fingers as she teased herself. Too much. He tried to hold back, but it was game over when she cried out as she shattered. The feel of her body milking his propelled him over the edge.

He snarled, clutched her tighter and thrust into her harder, faster, until she was through the haze of one orgasm and climbing towards the next with him. She rocked faster too, a wild little thing in his arms as she bounced on him, moaning with each deep plunge of his cock.

He tightened the fist in her hair, pushed it up the back of her head and exposed the nape of her neck.

A low growl rumbled through him.

The moonlight played across it, luring his eyes to it and keeping them there.

Gods, he needed to mark it.

He swooped on it, laved it with his tongue and shuddered as he tasted her.

The need to lick it seized him, jacked him higher and filled him with desperation, a deep and powerful urge that he couldn't quite sate or control as he stroked his tongue over her nape, drank her moans and whispered pleas.

He growled, held her harder and thrust deeper, but it wasn't enough to satisfy her.

It was a world away from satisfying him.

There was only one thing that would do that.

He laved her harder, trembled with each one as the fire in his belly spread lower and his balls tightened, tingling with each stroke of his tongue in time with every thrust of his cock into her.

He needed her.

Needed her to be his.

She needed him too.

Gods, he could feel it already.

He could feel her desperation, that wild need she didn't quite understand but that mastered her, had her writhing and rocking in his arms, trembling as violently as he was as she sought release that refused to come.

He would give it to her, to them both.

He pumped her deeper, harder still, unable to hold himself back. His tongue pressed hard into her nape with each stroke, each thrust, teasing her higher together with him, until he was at the precipice and couldn't go any higher, couldn't take it any longer.

"Talon," Sherry whispered.

A plea and permission all rolled into one.

On a feral growl, he sank his fangs into the back of her neck.

Her cry echoed around the forest, beat in his heart and warmed his soul.

He pulled her against him, plastered her back to his front and buried himself deep inside her as she shook, her body convulsing around his and pushing him over the edge with her. His entire body quaked from the force of his release as he throbbed and spilled inside her, and he fought to remain conscious as her emotions flowed into him, her joy and excitement, and her fear.

Talon closed his eyes and held her with his teeth, and in his arms, keeping her close to him and focusing as best he could so she would feel how much this meant to him.

How he would always be there for her, would be the one to take care of her now, and forever.

Because he was in love with her.

His beautiful mate.

She slowly began to relax against him, little by little sinking into him. He kept her pinned to him, unable to convince his body to do the same, needing to hold on to her. He was probably hurting her, hated that he might be, but his body and mind were ignoring his heart's attempts to calm them, screamed at him to keep her locked in his arms and in his teeth.

Her blood was warm on his tongue, tasted like honey and vanilla.

"Talon," she murmured, no trace of pain in her voice even though he knew she was hurting already, that the bliss of the moment was passing and she was growing aware of his fangs in her flesh, and her body as it began the first steps of her transformation.

His mate needed him.

She needed him to comfort her, to take away her pain and her fear.

Instinct as her mate seized him, more powerful than he had expected it to be, overpowering him.

His fangs were out of her flesh in a heartbeat, his tongue laving over the wounds to soothe them as his grip on her loosened.

She sighed and relaxed a little.

He purred like a fucking cub again, the pleasure that ran through him on realising he had satisfied her, his mate, stronger than any physical release, sweeter than anything he had ever experienced.

He kept purring as he licked her wounds, as she relaxed further and he felt her fear ebbing away, her pain fading.

She lifted her left hand, brushed his cheek with her fingers and then traced them over one of the wounds on the back of her neck. He drew back to give her space, a desire that lasted all of a second, obliterated by a need to crush her against his chest when he saw her fingers trembling and felt the flicker of fear ignite inside her again.

"Is it done?" she whispered.

Talon didn't stop her when she turned to face him, straddling his thighs. No fear touched her blue eyes. They were beautiful and mesmerising as they held his, filled with hope and excitement, and a fucking hell of a lot of love.

He nodded, raised his right hand and swept his knuckles across her cheek before opening his palm and cupping it as he stared into her eyes.

His mate.

"Soon, you'll be like me," he husked, thanking the gods for her and her courage, her strength, and humbled by what she had done for him, giving up her life as a mortal to step into his world.

Her lips curved into a slight smile that stole his breath. "A tiger."

He purred and wrapped his arms around her, held her closer so he could feel her heart beating against his. "My mate. My pride."

That smile grew a little wider as she looped her arms around his neck and leaned in, bringing her mouth close to his, and melted the heart she now held in her hands with her words.

Two whispered ones against his lips that told him everything she felt, and echoed his own feelings perfectly, showing him just how much they were meant to be.

That meeting her had been his destiny.

"Mine forever."

The End

ABOUT THE AUTHOR

Felicity Heaton is a New York Times and USA Today best-selling author who writes passionate paranormal romance books. In her books she creates detailed worlds, twisting plots, mind-blowing action, intense emotion and heart-stopping romances with leading men that vary from dark deadly vampires to sexy shape-shifters and wicked werewolves, to sinful angels and hot demons!

If you're a fan of paranormal romance authors Lara Adrian, J R Ward, Sherrilyn Kenyon, Gena Showalter, Larissa Ione and Christine Feehan then you will enjoy her books too.

If you love your angels a little dark and wicked, the best-selling Her Angel series is for you. If you like strong, powerful, and dark vampires then try the Vampires Realm series or any of her stand-alone vampire romance books. If you're looking for vampire romances that are sinful, passionate and erotic then try the best-selling Vampire Erotic Theatre series. Or if you prefer huge detailed worlds filled with hot-blooded alpha males in every species, from elves to demons to dragons to shifters and angels, then take a look at the new Eternal Mates series.

If you have enjoyed this story, please take a moment to contact the author at **author@felicityheaton.co.uk** or to post a review of the book online

Connect with Felicity:
Website – http://www.felicityheaton.co.uk
Blog – http://www.felicityheaton.co.uk/blog/
Twitter – http://twitter.com/felicityheaton
Facebook – http://www.facebook.com/felicityheaton
Goodreads – http://www.goodreads.com/felicityheaton
Mailing List – http://www.felicityheaton.co.uk/newsletter.php

FIND OUT MORE ABOUT HER BOOKS AT:
http://www.felicityheaton.co.uk